'Extravagantly strange in style and setting, it shows an author making a spectacular imaginative leap ... With uncanny mastery, Saunders encompasses aching emotion and macabre fantasy ... Prodigiously inventive, this is a novel that takes enormous risks' Peter Kemp, *Sunday Times*

'Saunders' extraordinary verbal energy is harnessed, for the most part, in the service of capturing the pathos of everyday life ... It is Saunders's beautifully realized portrait of Lincoln – caught at this hinge moment in time, in his own personal bardo, as it were – that powers this book' Michiko Kakutani, *New York Times*

'Moving and deeply felt ... And yet, somehow, there is always humour in this novel, as Saunders creates an invisible universe that is both terrible and wonderful. And, more than humour, there is that quality that Saunders has already told us he prizes so highly: kindness ... A great novel; a human cry for action – and compassion' Erica Wagner, *New Statesman*

'Truly strange and enchanting ... George Saunders concocts a narrative like no other ... Majestic and spellbinding' *Independent*

'Revelatory. In structure, execution and emotional force, *Lincoln* is a masterpiece – a tapestry of fact, counterfact and wild, hallucinatory invention ... A symphonic and deeply humanistic vision – a mapping of the bardo between truth and fiction that has, perhaps more than Saunders ever could have imagined as he was crafting this book, become our contemporary reality' Sam Byers, *Spectator*

'Along ... abounds in
Lincol ... o the dead.
Optimi ... al we carry
within ... . The book
was cl ... herworldly
love' *T*...

'A nuanced portrait of a conflicted American society, one that grapples with issues of race, regret and remembering ... An assured and ambitious debut novel from a prose stylist of rare imagination' *Daily Express*

'A surreal metaphysical drama about grief and freedom ... A father-son narrative that is both hilarious and haunting ... Saunders returns us to the world afresh with an idea that is both difficult and joyful: there is life before death' *Evening Standard*

'A strange and haunting novel ... about the effect the dead have on the living, and the living on the dead' *Economist*

'A wildly fanciful and at times close to unbearably moving tale of the supernatural ... Willie Lincoln will linger in the mind long after the others have faded' *Times Literary Supplement*

'A busy Greek chorus that ranges over death, slavery, sex, war, love, endless rue and the awful grief a child's death arouses. The writing constantly surprises' *Mail on Sunday*

'Saunders has achieved a mastery of effect that makes *Lincoln in the Bardo* so funny and sad as to wring both kinds of tears from your eyes' *Herald*

'Ingenious ... Saunders – well on his way toward becoming a twenty-first-century Twain – crafts an American patchwork of love and loss' *Vogue*

'The novel beats with a present-day urgency – a nation at war with itself, the unbearable grief of a father who has lost a child, and a howling congregation of ghosts' *Vanity Fair*

'A stunning depiction of the sixteenth President's psyche' *New Yorker*

'A brilliant, Buddhist reimagining of an American story of great loss and great love ... An unsentimental novel of Shakespearean proportions, gorgeously stuffed with tragic characters, bawdy humour, terrifying visions, throat-catching tenderness, and a galloping narrative' *Elle*

GEORGE SAUNDERS is the author of nine books, including *Tenth of December*, which was a finalist for the National Book Award and won the inaugural Folio Prize (for the best work of fiction in English) and the Story Prize (best short-story collection). He has received MacArthur and Guggenheim fellowships and the PEN/Malamud Prize for excellence in the short story, and was recently elected to the American Academy of Arts and Sciences. In 2013, he was named one of the world's 100 most influential people by *Time* magazine. He teaches in the creative writing program at Syracuse University.

georgesaundersbooks.com

BY GEORGE SAUNDERS

FICTION

CivilWarLand in Bad Decline

Pastoralia

The Very Persistent Gappers of Frip

The Brief and Frightening Reign of Phil

In Persuasion Nation

Tenth of December

Lincoln in the Bardo

NONFICTION

The Brain-Dead Megaphone

Congratulations, by the Way

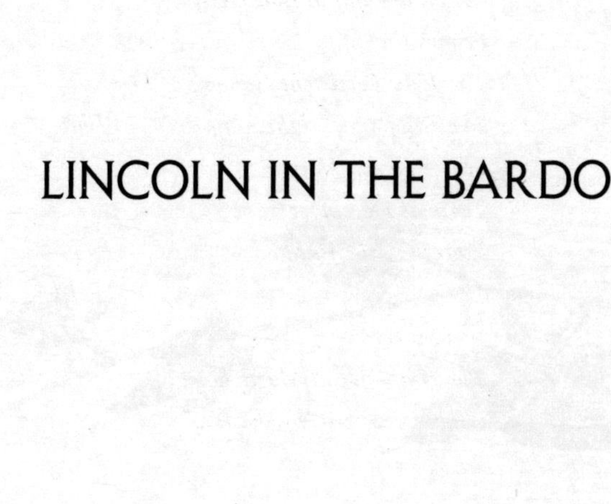

LINCOLN IN THE BARDO

LINCOLN IN THE BARDO

GEORGE SAUNDERS

BLOOMSBURY
LONDON · OXFORD · NEW YORK · NEW DELHI · SYDNEY

Bloomsbury Paperbacks
An imprint of Bloomsbury Publishing Plc

50 Bedford Square
London
WC1B 3DP
UK

1385 Broadway
New York
NY 10018
USA

www.bloomsbury.com

First published in Great Britain 2017
This paperback edition first published in 2017

British Library Cataloguing-in-Publication Data
A catalogue record for this book is available from the British Library.

ISBN:		
	HB:	978-1-4088-7174-4
	TPB:	978-1-4088-7175-1
	PB:	978-1-4088-7177-5
	ePub:	978-1-4088-7176-8

2 4 6 8 10 9 7 5 3 1

Book design by Greg Heinimann and Barbara M. Bachman
Printed and bound in Great Britain by CPI Group (UK) Ltd, Croydon CR0 4YY

To find out more about our authors and books visit www.bloomsbury.com. Here you will find extracts, author interviews, details of forthcoming events and the option to sign up for our newsletters.

For Caitlin and Alena

LINCOLN IN THE BARDO

ONE

I.

On our wedding day I was forty-six, she was eighteen. Now, I know what you are thinking: older man (not thin, somewhat bald, lame in one leg, teeth of wood) exercises the marital prerogative, thereby mortifying the poor young—

But that is false.

That is exactly what I refused to do, you see.

On our wedding night I clumped up the stairs, face red with drink and dance, found her arrayed in some thinnish thing an aunt had forced her into, silk collar fluttering slightly with her quaking—and could not do it.

Speaking to her softly, I told her my heart: she was beautiful; I was old, ugly, used up; this match was strange, had its roots not in love but expedience; her father was poor, her mother ill. That was why she was here. I knew all of this very well. And would not dream of touching her, I said, when I could see her fear and—the word I used was "distaste."

She assured me she did not feel "distaste" even as I saw her (fair, flushed) face distort with the lie.

I proposed that we should be . . . friends. Should behave outwardly, in all things, as if we had consummated our arrangement. She should feel relaxed and happy in my home and endeavor to make it her own. I would expect nothing more of her.

And that is how we lived. We became friends. Dear friends. That was all. And yet that was so much. We laughed together, made decisions about the household—she helped me bear the servants more in mind, speak to them less perfunctorily. She had a fine eye and accomplished a successful renovation of the rooms at a fraction of the expected cost. To see her brighten when I came in, find her leaning into me as we discussed some household matter, improved my lot in ways I cannot adequately explain. I had been happy, happy enough, but now I often found myself uttering a spontaneous prayer that went, simply: *She is here, still here.* It was as if a rushing river had routed itself through my house, which was pervaded now by a freshwater scent and the awareness of something lavish, natural, and breathtaking always moving nearby.

At dinner one evening, unprompted, before a group of my friends, she sang my praises—said I was a good man: thoughtful, intelligent, kind.

As our eyes met I saw that she had spoken in earnest.

Next day, she left a note on my desk. Although shyness prevented her from expressing this sentiment in speech or action, the note said, my kindness to her had resulted in an effect much to be desired: she was happy, was indeed comfortable in *our* home, and desired, as she put it, to "expand the frontiers of our happiness together in that intimate way to which I am, as yet, a stranger." She requested that I guide her in this as I had guided her "in so many other aspects of adulthood."

I read the note, went in to supper—found her positively aglow. We exchanged frank looks there in front of the servants, delighted by this thing we had somehow managed to make for ourselves from such unpromising materials.

That night, in her bed, I was careful not to be other than I had been: gentle, respectful, deferential. We did little—kissed, held one another—but imagine, if you will, the richness of this sudden indulgence. We both felt the rising tide of lust (yes, of course) but undergirded by the slow, solid affection we had built: a trustworthy bond, durable and genuine. I was not an inexperienced man—had been wild when young; had spent sufficient time (I am ashamed to say) in Marble Alley, at the Band-box, at the dreadful Wolf's Den; had been married once before, and healthily so—but the intensity of this feeling was altogether new to me.

It was tacitly understood that, next night, we would further explore this "new continent," and I went to my printing offices in the morning fighting the gravitational pull that bid me stay home.

And that day—alas—was the day of the beam.

Yes, yes, what luck!

A beam from the ceiling came down, hitting me just *here,* as I sat at my desk. And so our plan must be deferred, while I recovered. Per the advice of my physician, I took to my—

A sort of sick-box was judged—was judged to be—

hans vollman

Efficacious.

roger bevins iii

Efficacious, yes. Thank you, friend.

hans vollman

Always a pleasure.

roger bevins iii

There I lay, in my sick-box, feeling foolish, in the parlor, the very parlor through which we had recently (gleefully, guiltily, her hand in mine) passed en route to her bedroom. Then the physician returned, and his assistants carried my sick-box to his sick-cart, and I saw that—I saw that our plan must be indefinitely delayed. What a frustration! When, now, would I know the full pleasures of the marriage-bed; when behold her naked form; when would she turn to me in that certain state, mouth hungry, cheeks flushed; when would her hair, loosened in a wanton gesture, fall at last around us?

Well, it seemed we must wait until my recovery was complete.

A vexing development indeed.

hans vollman

And yet all things may be borne.

roger bevins iii

Quite so.

Although I confess I was not of that mind at the time. At that time, there on the sick-cart, as yet unbound, I found I could briefly leave my sick-box, darting out and causing little duststorms, and even cracked a vase, a vase on the porch. But my wife and that physician, earnestly discussing my injury, did not notice. I could not abide it. And threw a bit of a tantrum, I admit, and sent the dogs yipping away, by passing through them and inducing in each a dream of a bear. I could do that then! Those were the days! Now I could no more induce a dream of a bear in a dog than I could take our silent young friend here out to dinner!

(He does appear young, doesn't he, Mr. Bevins? In his contours? His posture?)

In any event, I returned to my sick-box, weeping in that way that we have—have you come to know this yet, young fellow? When we are newly arrived in this hospital-yard, young sir, and feel like weeping, what happens is, we tense up ever so slightly, and there is a mildly toxic feeling in the joints, and little things inside us burst. Sometimes we might poop a bit if we are fresh. Which is just what I did, out on the cart that day: I pooped a bit while fresh, in my sick-box, out of rage, and what was the result? I have kept that poop with me all this time, and as a matter of fact—I hope you do not find this rude, young sir, or off-putting, I hope it does not impair our nascent friendship—that poop is still down there, at this moment, in my sick-box, albeit much dryer!

Goodness, are you a child?

He is, isn't he?

hans vollman

I believe so. Now that you mention it.

Here he comes.

Nearly fully formed now.

roger bevins iii

My apologies. Good God. To be confined to a sick-box while still a child—and have to listen to an adult detailing the presence of a dried poop in his sick-box—is not exactly the, uh, ideal way to make one's entree into a new, ah—

A boy. A mere lad. Oh dear.

Many apologies.

hans vollman

II.

"You know," Mrs. Lincoln said to me, "The President is expected to give a series of state dinners every winter, and these dinners are very costly. If I give three large receptions, the state dinners can be scratched from the programme. If I can make Mr. Lincoln take the same view of the case, I shall not fail to put the idea into practice."

"I believe you are right," said the President. "You argue your point well. I think that we shall have to decide upon the receptions."

The question was decided, and arrangements were made for the first reception.

In "Behind the Scenes or Thirty Years a Slave and Four Years in the White House," by Elizabeth Keckley.

Abolitionists criticized the merry-making at the White House and many declined to attend. Ben Wade's regrets were said to have been harshly worded: "Are the President and Mrs. Lincoln aware that there is a civil war? If they are not, Mr. and Mrs. Wade are, and for that reason decline to participate in feasting and dancing."

In "Reveille in Washington, 1860–1865," by Margaret Leech.

The children, Tad and Willie, were constantly receiving presents. Willie was so delighted with a little pony, that he insisted on riding it every day. The weather was changeable, and exposure resulted in a severe cold, which deepened into fever.

Keckley, op. cit.

Willie was burning with fever on the night of the fifth, as his mother dressed for the party. He drew every breath with difficulty. She could see that his lungs were congested and she was frightened.

In "Twenty Days," by Dorothy Meserve Kunhardt and Philip B. Kunhardt Jr.

III.

[The Lincolns'] party had been savagely attacked, but all the important people had come to it.

Leech, op. cit.

A clear sightline could not be obtained for the crush; one moved dazed through a veritable bazaar of scents, colognes, perfumes, fans, hairpieces, hats, grimacing faces, mouths held open in sudden shrieks, whether joyful or terrified it was difficult to say.

In "All This Did I See: Memories of a Terrible Time," by Mrs. Margaret Garrett.

Exotic flowers from the presidential greenhouse were in vases every few yards.

Kunhardt and Kunhardt, op. cit.

The diplomatic corps made a brilliant group—Lord Lyons, M. Mercier, M. Stoeckl, M. von Limburg, Senor Tassara, Count Piper, Chevalier Bertinatti, and the rest.

Leech, op. cit.

Multitiered chandeliers illuminated the East Room, above carpets of sea-foam green.

In "Rise to Greatness," by David Von Drehle.

A patter of languages sounded in the Blue Room, where General McDowell, conversing in perfect French, was made much of by the Europeans.

Leech, op. cit.

Every nation, race, rank, age, height, breadth, voice-pitch, hairstyle, posture, and fragrance seemed represented: a rainbow come to life, calling out in manifold accents.

Garrett, op. cit.

There were Cabinet members, senators, representatives, distinguished citizens and beautiful women from nearly every State. Few army officers were present below the rank of division commander. The French princes had come, and Prince Felix Salm-Salm, a Prussian nobleman and cavalry officer who was serving on General Blenker's staff . . .

Leech, op. cit.

. . . the dashing German, Salum-Salum; the Whitney brothers (twins and indistinguishable except that one wore a captain's ribbons and the other those of a lieutenant); Ambassador Thorn-Tooley; Mr. & Mrs. Fessenden; the novelist E.D.E.N. Southworth; George Francis Train and his beautiful wife ("half his age, twice his height," ran a witticism popular at the time).

Garrett, op. cit.

Nearly lost among a huge flower arrangement stood a clutch of bent old men in urgent discussion, heads centrally inclined. These were Abernathy, Seville, and Kord, all of whom would be dead within the year. The Casten sisters, terrifically tall and pale, stood at a slant nearby, like alabaster anthers seeking light, attempting to overhear the conversation.

In "The Union Citadel: Memories and Impressions," by Jo Brunt.

Before them all, at eleven o'clock, Mrs. Lincoln led the promenade around the East Room on the President's arm.

Leech, op. cit.

As we surged forward, a man unknown to me demonstrated a new dance, the "Merry-Jim." At the urging of those gathered around, he demonstrated it again, to applause.

Garrett, op. cit.

There was great hilarity when it was discovered that a servant had locked the door of the state dining-room, and misplaced the key. "I am in favor of a forward movement!" cried one. "An advance to the front is only retarded by the imbecility of commanders," said another, parroting a recent speech in Congress.

Leech, op. cit.

This, it occurred to me, this was the undisciplined human community that, fired by its dull collective wit, now drove the armed nation towards it knew-not-what sort of epic martial cataclysm: a massive flailing organism with all the rectitude and foresight of an untrained puppy.

In the private letters of Albert Sloane, by permission of the Sloane family.

The war was less than a year old. We did not yet know what it was.

In "A Thrilling Youth: A Civil War Adolescence," by E. G. Frame.

When at last the key was found, and the merry guests poured in, Mrs. Lincoln had reason for pride in the magnificence of the repast.

Leech, op. cit.

The room was forty feet long by thirty feet wide, and so bright with color it seemed to be full before anyone entered.

In "The Lincolns: Portrait of a Marriage,"
by Daniel Mark Epstein.

Costly wines and liquors flowed freely, and the immense Japanese punch bowl was filled with ten gallons of champagne punch.

Leech, op. cit.

Mrs. Lincoln had engaged the esteemed caterer C. Heerdt of New York. The cost was rumored to be over ten thousand dollars. Nor had any detail been overlooked; the chandeliers were garlanded with flowers, the serving tables decorated with rose petals scattered over cut rectangles of mirror.

Brunt, op. cit.

A piggish and excessive display, in a time of war.

Sloane, op. cit.

Elsa was speechless and only kept squeezing my hand. In such a way, one felt, the ancients must have entertained. What generosity! How kind our dear hosts!

In "Our Capital in Time of War,"
by Petersen Wickett.

In the dining room was a long table with a gigantic looking-glass upon it bearing massive confections of sugar. Most recognizable were Fort Sumter, a warship, a temple of liberty, a Chinese pagoda, a Swiss cottage . . .

Kunhardt and Kunhardt, op. cit.

. . . sweetened replicas of a temple surrounded by the Goddess of Liberty, Chinese pagodas, cornucopias, fountains with sprays of spun sugar and encircled by stars . . .

In "Mr. Lincoln's Washington,"
by Stanley Kimmel.

Hives, swarming with lifelike bees, were filled with charlotte russe. War was gently hinted at by a helmet, with waving plumes of spun sugar. The good American frigate "Union," with forty guns and all sails set, was supported by cherubs draped in the Stars and Stripes . . .

Leech, op. cit.

Fort Pickens also loomed up in sugar on a side table, surrounded by something more edible than barbette guns, in the shape of a deliciously prepared "chicken fixin's" . . .

Kimmel, op. cit.

The flowing sugar gown of Lady Liberty descended like drapery upon a Chinese pagoda, inside of which, in a pond of candy floss, swam miniature fish of chocolate. Nearby, lusty angels of cake waved away bees hung aloft on the thinnest strings of glaze.

Wickett, op. cit.

At first delicate and perfect, over the course of the night this candy metropolis suffered various ravages, members of the party taking away entire quarters of the city in fists, into pockets, to share with loved ones at home. Later in the evening, the glass table being jostled by the crush, certain of the candied edifices were seen to give way.

Garrett, op. cit.

They dined on tender pheasant, fat partridge, venison steaks, and Virginia hams; they battened upon canvasback ducks and fresh turkeys, and thousands of tidewater oysters shucked an hour since and iced, slurped raw, scalloped in butter and crackermeal, or stewed in milk.

Epstein, op. cit.

These, and other tasty morsels, were spread about in such profusion that the joint attack of the thousand or more guests failed to deplete the array.

Kimmel, op. cit.

Yet there was no joy in the evening for the mechanically smiling hostess and her husband. They kept climbing the stairs to see how Willie was, and he was not doing well at all.

Kunhardt and Kunhardt, op. cit.

IV.

The rich notes of the Marine Band in the apartments below came to the sick-room in soft, subdued murmurs, like the wild, faint sobbing of far-off spirits.

Keckley, op. cit.

Willie lay in the "Prince of Wales" bedroom with its dark purple wall hangings and golden tassels.

Epstein, op. cit.

The cheeks of his handsome round face were inflamed with fever. His feet moved restlessly beneath the maroon coverlet.

In "History Close at Hand," edited by
Renard Kent, account of Mrs. Kate O'Brien.

The terror and consternation of the Presidential couple may be imagined by anyone who has ever loved a child, and suffered that dread intimation common to all parents, that Fate may not hold that life in as high a regard, and may dispose of it at will.

In "Selected Civil War Letters of
Edwine Willow," edited by Constance Mays.

With Fear clutching at their hearts, they went downstairs once more to hear the singers of the evening, the Hutchison family, give a frighteningly real rendition of the song "Ship on Fire," which required simulation of a violent thunderstorm at sea, the frightened screams of the trapped passengers, a mother pressing her babe to her bosom of snow, "a tramp, a rout, an uproar of voices—'Fire! Fire!' "

The cheeks of the sailors grew pale
at the sight—and their eyes glistened with the gleam
of the light—and the smoke in thick wreaths mounted
higher and higher—Oh God it is fearful to perish by fire!

Kunhardt and Kunhardt, op. cit.

The noise and clatter were such that to be understood it was necessary to shout. Carriages continued to arrive. Windows were thrown open and groups formed around them, hoping for a gust of chill night air. An air of happy panic pervaded the room. I began to feel faint and believe I was not alone in this. Matrons were collapsed here and there in armchairs. Drunken men examined paintings rather too intensely.

Garrett, op. cit.

Wild shrieks rang out.

Sloane, op. cit.

One fellow stood in perfect happiness, orange-trousered, blue coat flung open, feasting in-place as he stood at the serving table like some magnificent Ambrussi, finally found the home of his dreams.

Wickett, op. cit.

The flower arrangements of history! Those towering bursts of colors, so lavish—soon tossed away, to dry and go drab in the dim February sun. The animal carcasses—the "meat"—warm and sprig-covered, on expensive platters, steaming and succulent: trucked away to who-knows-where, clearly offal now, honest partial corpses once again, after brief elevation to the status of delight-giving food! The thousand dresses, laid out so reverently that afternoon, flecks of dust brushed off carefully in doorways, hems gathered up for the carriage trip: where are they now? Is a single one museum-displayed? Are some few yet saved in attics? Most are dust. As are the women who wore them so proudly in that transient moment of radiance.

In "The Social Life of the Civil War: Frolic, Carnage, Extirpation" (unpublished manuscript), by Melvin Carter.

V.

Many guests especially recalled the beautiful moon that shone that evening.

In "A Season of War and Loss,"
by Ann Brighney.

In several accounts of the evening, the brilliance of the moon is remarked upon.

In "Long Road to Glory," by Edward Holt.

A common feature of these narratives is the golden moon, hanging quaintly above the scene.

In "White House Soirees: An Anthology,"
by Bernadette Evon.

There was no moon that night and the sky was heavy with clouds.

Wickett, op. cit.

A fat green crescent hung above the mad scene like a stolid judge, inured to all human folly.

In "My Life," by Dolores P. Leventrop.

The full moon that night was yellow-red, as if reflecting the light of some earthly fire.

Sloane, op. cit.

As I moved about the room I would encounter that silver wedge of a moon at this window or that, like some old beggar who wished to be invited in.

Carter, op. cit.

By the time dinner was served, the moon shone high and small and blue above, still bright, albeit somewhat diminished.

In "A Time Departed" (unpublished memoir), by I. B. Brigg III.

The night continued dark and moonless; a storm was moving in.

In "Those Most Joyful Years," by Albert Trundle.

The guests began to depart as the full yellow moon hung among morning stars.

In "The Washington Powers," by D. V. Featherly.

The clouds were heavy, leaden, and low, of a dull roseate color. There was no moon. My husband and I paused to look up at the room in which young Lincoln suffered. I said a silent prayer for the health of the lad. We found the carriage and made for home, where our own children, thanks be to a merciful God, were resting peacefully.

In "One Mother Remembers," by Abigail Service.

VI.

The last guests lingered almost until dawn. In the basement, servants worked all night to clean up, drinking leftover wine as they toiled. Hot, tired, and drunk, several of them began arguing, which led to a fistfight in the kitchen.

Von Drehle, op. cit.

I heard it said several times, in hushed whispers: it was wrong to engage in such merry-making when Death itself had made itself known at the door, and perhaps the more modest the public life at such a time, the more apposite.

In "Collected Wartime Letters of Barbara Smith-Hill," edited by Thomas Schofield and Edward Moran.

The night passed slowly; morning came, and Willie was worse.

Keckley, op. cit.

VII.

Yesterday around three there came a considerable procession—perhaps twenty carriages and nowhere to put them—They stopped on the lawns of the houses and sat aslant on the cemetery land by the fence—And who should alight from the hearse but Mr. L. himself, whom I could recognize from his likeness—But sore bent down and sad in countenance, almost needing to be urged along, as if reluctant to enter that drear place—I had not yet heard the sad news & was momentarily puzzled but soon enough the situation being made clear I prayed for the boy & family—it has been much in the papers regarding his illness and it has had the unhappy outcome now—The carriages cont'd to arrive over the next hour until the street was impassable.

The large crowd disappeared inside the chapel and from my open window I could hear the proceedings within: music, a sermon, weeping. Then the gathering dispersed & the carriages moved off, several becoming stuck & requiring unsticking, the street & lawns being left a considerable mess.

Then today, again wet & cold, and, around two, a single small carriage arrived & stopped at the cemetery gate & again the President got out, this time accompanied by three gentlemen: one young & two OLD.—they were met at the gate by Mr. Weston & his young assistant & all went off to the chapel—Before long, the assistant being joined by a helper, they were seen to be managing a small coffin on to a handcart & off the sad party went, cart in the lead, the President & his companions plodding along behind—their destination appeared to be to the northwest corner of the cemetery. The hill there being steep and the rain continuing, it made a strange joining of somber melancholy & riotous awkwardness, the assistants struggling to keep the tiny coffin upon the cart—& at the same time all parties, even Mr. L., diligently mincing to maintain their footing on the rainslick grass.

Anyway it appears the poor Lincoln child is to be left there across the road, contrary to reports in the newspapers, which ventured that he would be returning to Illinois forthwith. They have been loaned a place in the crypt belonging to Judge Carroll, & only imagine the pain of that, Andrew, to drop one's precious son into that cold stone like some broken bird & be on your way.

Quiet tonight, & even the Creek seems to murmur along more quietly than usual, dear Brother. The moon came out just now & lit the stones in the cemetery—for an instant it appeared the grounds had been overrun with angels of various shapes and sizes: fat angels, dog-sized angels, angels upon horseback, etc.

I have grown comfortable having these Dead for company, and find them agreeable companions, over there in their Soil & cold stone Houses.

In "Wartime Washington: The Civil War Letters of Isabelle Perkins," compiled and edited by Nash Perkins III, entry of February 25, 1862.

VIII.

So the President left his boy in a loaned tomb and went back to his work for the country.

In "Lincoln: A Story for Boys,"
by Maxwell Flagg.

Nothing could have been more peaceful or more beautiful than the situation of this tomb and it was completely undiscoverable to the casual cemetery visitor, being the very last tomb on the left at the extreme far reaches of the grounds, at the top of an almost perpendicular hillside that descended to Rock Creek below. The rapid water made a pleasant rushing sound and the forest trees stood up bare and strong against the sky.

Kunhardt and Kunhardt, op. cit.

IX.

Early in my youth I found I had a certain predilection which, to me, felt quite natural and even wonderful, but to others—my father, mother, brothers, friends, teachers, clergy, grandparents—my predilection did not seem natural or wonderful at all, but perverse and shameful, and hence I suffered: must I deny my predilection, and marry, and doom myself to a certain, shall we say, dearth of fulfillment? I wished to be happy (as I believe all wish to be happy), and so undertook an innocent—well, a *rather* innocent—friendship with a fellow in my school. But we soon saw that there was no hope for us, and so (to race past a few details, and stops-and-starts, and fresh beginnings, and heartfelt resolutions, and betrayals of those resolutions, there, in one corner of the, ah, carriage house, and so on), one afternoon, a day or so after a particularly frank talk, in which Gilbert stated his intention to henceforth "live correctly," I took a butcher knife to my room and, after writing a note to my parents (*I am sorry,* was the gist), and another to him (*I have loved, and therefore depart fulfilled*), I slit my wrists rather savagely over a porcelain tub.

Feeling nauseous at the quantity of blood and its sudden percussive redness against the whiteness of the tub, I settled myself woozily down on the floor, at which time I—well, it is a little embarrassing, but let me just say it: I *changed my mind.* Only then (nearly out the door, so to speak) did I realize how unspeakably *beautiful* all of this was, how precisely engineered for our pleasure, and saw that I was on the brink of squandering a wondrous gift, the gift of being allowed, every day, to wander this vast sensual paradise, this grand marketplace lovingly stocked with every sublime thing: swarms of insects dancing in slant-rays of August sun; a trio of black horses standing hock-deep and head-to-head in a field of snow; a waft of beef broth arriving breeze-borne from an orange-hued window on a chill autumn—

roger bevins iii

Sir. Friend.

hans vollman

Am I—am I doing it again?

roger bevins iii

You are.

Take a breath. All is well.

I believe you are somewhat alarming our new arrival.

hans vollman

Many apologies, young sir. I only meant, in my way, to welcome you.

roger bevins iii

Feeling "nauseous at the quantity of blood," you "settled yourself woozily down on the floor" and "changed your mind."

hans vollman

Yes.

Feeling nauseous at the quantity of blood and its sudden percussive redness against the whiteness of the tub, I settled myself woozily down on the floor. At which time I *changed my mind*.

Knowing that my only hope was to be found by one of the servants, I stumbled to the stairs and threw myself down. From there, I managed to crawl into the kitchen—

Which is where I remain.

I am waiting to be discovered (having come to rest on the floor, head against the stove, upended chair nearby, sliver of an orange peel against my cheek), so that I may be revived, and rise, and clean up the awful mess I have made (Mother will *not* be pleased), and go outside, into that beautiful world, a new and more courageous man, and begin to *live*! Will I follow my predilection? I will! With gusto! Having come so close to losing everything, I am freed now of all fear, hesitation, and timidity, and, once revived, intend to devoutly wander the earth, imbibing, smelling, sampling, loving whomever I please; touching, tasting, standing very still among the beautiful things of this world, such as, for example: a sleeping dog dream-kicking in a tree-shade triangle; a sugar pyramid upon a blackwood tabletop being rearranged grain-by-grain by an indiscernible draft; a cloud passing ship-like above a rounded green hill, atop which a line of colored shirts energetically dance in the wind, while down below in town, a purple-blue day unfolds (the muse of spring incarnate), each moist-grassed, flower-pierced yard gone positively mad with—

roger bevins iii

Friend.

Bevins.

hans vollman

"Bevins" had several sets of eyes   All darting to and fro   Several noses   All sniffing   His hands (he had multiple sets of hands, or else his hands were so quick they seemed to be many) struck this way and that, picking things up, bringing them to his face with a most inquisitive

Little bit scary

In telling his story he had grown so many extra eyes and noses and hands that his body all but vanished   Eyes like grapes on a vine   Hands feeling the eyes   Noses smelling the hands

Slashes on every one of the wrists.

willie lincoln

The newcomer sat on the roof of his sick-house, staring down in wonder at Mr. Bevins.

hans vollman

Occasionally stealing an amazed glance over at you, sir. At your considerable—

roger bevins iii

Come now, no need to speak of—

hans vollman

The other man (the one hit by a beam)   Quite naked   Member swollen to the size of   Could not take my eyes off

It bounced as he

Body like a dumpling   Broad flat nose like a sheep's

Quite naked indeed

Awful dent in the head   How could he walk around and talk with such a nasty—

willie lincoln

Presently we found ourselves joined by the Reverend Everly Thomas.

hans vollman

Who arrived, as he always arrives, at a hobbling sprint, eyebrows arched high, looking behind himself anxiously, hair sticking straight up, mouth in a perfect O of terror. And yet spoke, as he always speaks, with the utmost calmness and good sense.

roger bevins iii

A newcomer? said the Reverend.

I believe we have the honor of addressing a Mr. Carroll, Mr. Bevins said.

The lad only looked at us blankly.

hans vollman

The newcomer was a boy of some ten or eleven years. A handsome little fellow, blinking and gazing cautiously about him.

the reverend everly thomas

Resembling a fish who, having washed ashore, lies immobile and alert, acutely aware of its vulnerability.

hans vollman

Putting me in mind of a nephew of mine who had once fallen through the ice of the river and come home chilled to the bone. Fearful of his punishment, he had not the nerve to step inside; I found him leaning against the door for what warmth he could gain in that way, stunned, guilty, nearly insensate with cold.

roger bevins iii

No doubt you are feeling a certain pull? Mr. Vollman said. An urge? To go? Somewhere? More comfortable?

I feel I am to wait, the boy said.

It speaks! said Mr. Bevins.

the reverend everly thomas

Wait for what? Mr. Sheep-Dumpling said.

My mother, I said. My father. They will come shortly. To collect me

Mr. Sheep-Dumpling shook his head sadly His member also shook Sadly

They may come, said the many-eyed man. But I doubt they will collect you.

Then all three laughed With much clapping of the many-eyed man's many hands And waggling of Mr. Sheep-Dumpling's swollen member Even the Reverend laughed Though, laughing, he still looked frightened

In any event, they will not stay long, said Mr. Sheep-Dumpling.

All the while wishing themselves elsewhere, said the many-eyed man.

Thinking only of lunch, said the Reverend.

It is soon to be spring   The Christmas toys barely played with   I have a glass soldier whose head can turn   The epaulettes interchangeable   Soon flowers will bloom   Lawrence from the garden shed will give us each a cup of seeds

I am to wait   I said

willie lincoln

X.

I shot Mr. Bevins a look.

hans vollman

These young ones are not meant to tarry.

roger bevins iii

Matthison, *Aged Nine Years*? Tarried less than thirty minutes. Then dispersed with a small fartlike pop. Dwyer, *6 yrs & 5 mos*? Was not in the sick-box upon its arrival. Had apparently vacated in transit. Sullivan, *Infant*, tarried twelve or thirteen minutes, a crawling squalling ball of frustrated light. Russo, *Taken in Her Sixth Year, & Light of a Mother's Eye*? Tarried a mere four minutes. Looking behind stone after stone. "I am investigating after my schoolbook."

hans vollman

Poor dear.

the reverend everly thomas

The Evans twins, *Departed This Sorry Vale Together at 15 Years, 8 Months,* tarried nine minutes, then left at precisely the same instant (twins to the end). Percival Strout, *Aged Seventeen Years*, tarried forty minutes. Sally Burgess, *12 Years & Dear to All,* tarried seventeen minutes.

hans vollman

Belinda French, *Baby*. Remember her?

roger bevins iii

The size of a loaf of bread, and just lay there, giving off a dull white light and that high-pitched keening.

the reverend everly thomas

For fifty-seven straight minutes.

hans vollman

Long after her mother, Amanda French, *Lost Bringing Life to a Fair & Yet Unlucky Childe*, had gone on.

roger bevins iii

They lay together in a single sick-box.

hans vollman

A most touching sight.

the reverend everly thomas

But in time, she went.

roger bevins iii

As these young ones should.

the reverend everly thomas

As most do, quite naturally.

roger bevins iii

Or else.

the reverend everly thomas

Imagine our surprise, then, when, passing by an hour or so later, we found the lad still on the roof, looking expectantly about, as if waiting for a carriage to arrive and whisk him away.

hans vollman

And pardon me for saying so—but that wild-onion stench the young exude when tarrying? Was quite thick already.

roger bevins iii

Something needed to be done.

the reverend everly thomas

XI.

Walk with us, lad, Mr. Sheep-Dumpling said. There is someone we would like you to meet.

Can you walk? said the many-eyed man.

I found that I could

Could walk   Could skim   Could even walk-skim

A little walk-skim was bully by me   Something was lying untoward below us, in a box inside that little house

Untoward   ly

May I tell you something?

It had the face of a worm

A worm, I say!   A worm the size of a boy   Wearing my suit

Horrors.

willie lincoln

The lad made as if to take my hand, then seemed to think better of it, perhaps not wishing me to think him childish.

hans vollman

And we set off, making our way east.

roger bevins iii

XII.

Hello, kind sirs. If you wish, I can tell you the names of some of our wildwoods flowers?

mrs. elizabeth crawford

Mrs. Crawford fell in behind us, assuming her customary posture of extreme obeisance: bowing, smiling, scraping, flinching.

roger bevins iii

Thare is, for example, the wild sweet William, wild pink ladyslipper, wild roses of all types. Thare is butterfly weed, thare is huny suckle, and not to menshun blue flag, yellow flag, and A grate many other kinds that I cant recollect the Names of at this time.

mrs. elizabeth crawford

Being harassed all the while by Longstreet, that wretch who resides near the askew bench.

roger bevins iii

Mark you, gentlemen, my subtle understanding of the significant aspects of the costuming: the hooks-and-eyes, the Ellis-In, the intricate Rainy Daisy skirt, I tell you, Scudder, it's like peeling an onion: unlacing, unhooking, cajoling, until one gets, at last, hardly at a fast pace, to the center of the drama, the jewel—as one would say—its bosky dell—

sam "smooth-boy" longstreet

Who groped and pawed her continually as we went along, Mrs. Crawford remaining blessedly oblivious to his disgusting attentions.

the reverend everly thomas

The lad, overawed, followed close behind us, looking this way and that.

hans vollman

Well now I will give you A part of, or all of, if you like it, a Song my dear husband used to sing. Cauld it Adam and Eaves wedding Song. This Song was Sung by him at my sister's wedding. He was much in the habit of making Songs and Singing of them and—

Oh no, I won't go no closer.

Good day to you, sirs.

mrs. elizabeth crawford

We had reached the edge of an uninhabited wilderness of some several hundred yards that ended in the dreaded iron fence.

hans vollman

That noxious limit beyond which we could not venture.

roger bevins iii

How we hated the thing.

hans vollman

The Traynor girl lay as usual, trapped against, and part of, the fence, manifesting at that moment as a sort of horrid blackened furnace.

roger bevins iii

I could not help but recall her first day here, when she uninterruptedly manifested as a spinning young girl in a summer frock of continually shifting color.

the reverend everly thomas

I called out to her and asked her to speak to the lad. About the perils of this place. For the young.

hans vollman

The girl was silent. The door of the furnace she was at that moment only opened, then closed, affording us a brief glimpse of the terrible orange place of heat within.

roger bevins iii

She rapidly transmuted into the fallen bridge, the vulture, the large dog, the terrible hag gorging on black cake, the stand of flood-ravaged corn, the umbrella ripped open by a wind we could not feel.

the reverend everly thomas

Our earnest pleadings did no good. The girl would not talk.

hans vollman

We turned to go.

roger bevins iii

Something about the lad had touched her. The umbrella became the corn; the corn the hag; the hag the girl.

hans vollman

She gestured for him to step forward.

roger bevins iii

The lad approaching cautiously, she began to speak in a low voice we could not hear.

hans vollman

XIII.

Younge Mr Bristol desired me, younge Mr Fellowes and Mr Delway desired me, of an evening they would sit on the grass around me and in their eyes burned the fiercest kindest Desire. In my grape smock I would sit in the wikker chair amid that circle of admiring fierce kind eyes even unto the night when one or another boy would lay back and say, Oh the stars, and I would say, O yes, how fine they look tonight, while (I admit) imagining reclining there beside him, and the other boys, seeing me looking at the reklining one, would also imagine going down to recline there beside me.

It was all very

Then Mother would send Annie to come get me.

I was too early departed. From that party, from that

Brite promise of nights and nights of that, culminating in a choise, and the choise being made, it would be rite, and would become Love, and Love would become baby, and that is all I ask

I want ed so much to hold a dear Babe.

I know very wel I do not look as prety as I onseh. And over time, I admit, I have come to know serten words I did not formerly

Fuk cok shit reem ravage assfuk

And to know, in my mind, serten untoward kwarters where such things

Dim rum swoggling plases off bakalleys

Kome to love them

Crave them plases. And feel such anger.

I did not get any. Thing.

Was gone too soon

To get
Only forteen.
Yrs of aje
Plese do come again sir it has been a pleasure to make your

But fuk yr anshient frends (do not bring them agin) who kome to ogle and mok me and ask me to swindle no that is not the werd slender slander that wich I am doing. Wich is no more than what they are doing. Is it not so? What I am doing, if I only cary on fathefully, will, I am sure, bring about that longed-for return to

Green grass kind looks.

elise traynor

XIV.

Leaving that place the lad went quiet.

That will happen to me? he said.

It most certainly will, Mr. Vollman said.

It is—it is somewhat happening already, the Reverend added delicately.

roger bevins iii

We had reached the place where the dirt path drops down.

the reverend everly thomas

Near Freeley. Near Stevens. Near the four infant Nesbitts and their head-bent Angel.

roger bevins iii

Near Masterton. Near Ambusti. Near the obelisk and the three benches and the high-mounted bust of arrogant Merridale.

hans vollman

I believe, then, that I must do as you say, the boy said.

Good lad, said Mr. Vollman.

roger bevins iii

XV.

We embraced the boy at the door of his white stone home.

hans vollman

He gave us a shy smile, not untouched by trepidation at what was to come.

the reverend everly thomas

Go on, Mr. Bevins said gently. It is for the best.

hans vollman

Off you go, Mr. Vollman said. Nothing left for you here.

roger bevins iii

Goodbye then, the lad said.
Nothing scary about it, Mr. Bevins said. Perfectly natural.

hans vollman

Then it happened.

roger bevins iii

An extraordinary occurrence.

hans vollman

Unprecedented, really.

the reverend everly thomas

The boy's gaze moved past us.

hans vollman

He seemed to catch sight of something beyond.

roger bevins iii

His face lit up with joy.

hans vollman

Father, he said.

the reverend everly thomas

XVI.

An exceedingly tall and unkempt fellow was making his way toward us through the darkness.

hans vollman

This was highly irregular. It was after hours; the front gate would be locked.

the reverend everly thomas

The boy had been delivered only that day. That is to say, the man had most likely been here—

roger bevins iii

Quite recently.

hans vollman

That afternoon.

roger bevins iii

Highly irregular.

the reverend everly thomas

The gentleman seemed lost. Several times he stopped, looked about, retraced his steps, reversed course.

hans vollman

He was softly sobbing.

roger bevins iii

He was not sobbing. My friend remembers incorrectly. He was winded. He did not sob.

hans vollman

He was softly sobbing, his sadness aggravated by his mounting frustration at being lost.

roger bevins iii

He moved stiffly, all elbows and knees.

the reverend everly thomas

Bursting out of the doorway, the lad took off running toward the man, look of joy on his face.

roger bevins iii

Which turned to consternation when the man failed to sweep him up in his arms as, one gathered, must have been their custom.

the reverend everly thomas

The boy instead passing through the man, as the man continued to walk toward the white stone home, sobbing.

roger bevins iii

He was not sobbing. He was very much under control and moved with great dignity and certainty of—

hans vollman

He was fifteen yards away now, headed directly toward us.

roger bevins iii

The Reverend suggested we yield the path.

hans vollman

The Reverend having strong feelings about the impropriety of allowing oneself to be passed through.

roger bevins iii

The man reached the white stone home and let himself in with a key, the lad then following him in.

hans vollman

Mr. Bevins, Mr. Vollman, and I, concerned for the boy's welfare, moved into the doorway.

the reverend everly thomas

The man then did something—I do not quite know how to—

hans vollman

He was a large fellow. Quite strong, apparently. Strong enough to be able to slide the boy's—

the reverend everly thomas

Sick-box.

hans vollman

The man slid the box out of the slot in the wall, and set it down upon the floor.

roger bevins iii

And opened it.

hans vollman

Kneeling before the box, the man looked down upon that which—

the reverend everly thomas

He looked down upon the lad's prone form in the sick-box.

hans vollman

Yes.

the reverend everly thomas

At which point, he sobbed.

hans vollman

He had been sobbing all along.

roger bevins iii

He emitted a single, heartrending sob.

hans vollman

Or gasp. I heard it as more of a gasp. A gasp of recognition.

the reverend everly thomas

Of recollection.

hans vollman

Of suddenly remembering what had been lost.

the reverend everly thomas

And touched the face and hair fondly.

hans vollman

As no doubt he had many times done when the boy was—

roger bevins iii

Less sick.

hans vollman

A gasp of recognition, as if to say: Here he is again, my child, just as he was. I have found him again, he who was so dear to me.

the reverend everly thomas

Who was still so dear.

hans vollman

Yes.

roger bevins iii

The loss having been quite recent.

the reverend everly thomas

XVII.

Willie Lincoln was wasting away.

Epstein, op. cit.

The days dragged wearily by, and he grew weaker and more shadow-like.

Keckley, op. cit.

Lincoln's secretary, William Stoddard, recalled the question on everyone's lips: "Is there no hope? Not any. So the doctors say."

In "Team of Rivals: The Political Genius of Abraham Lincoln," by Doris Kearns Goodwin.

At about 5 o'clock this afternoon, I was lying half asleep on the sofa in my office, when his entrance aroused me. "Well, Nicolay," said he choking with emotion, "my boy is gone—he is actually gone!" and bursting into tears, turned and went into his own office.

In "With Lincoln in the White House," by John G. Nicolay, edited by Michael Burlingame.

The death was only moments ago. The body lay upon the bed, the coverlet thrown back. He wore the pale blue pajamas. His arms lay at his sides. The cheeks were still enflamed. Three pillows lay in a heap on the floor. The small side table was askew, as if roughly pushed aside.

In "Eyewitness to History: The Lincoln White House," edited by Stone Hilyard, account of Sophie Lenox, maid.

I assisted in washing him and dressing him, and then laid him on the bed, when Mr. Lincoln came in. I never saw a man so bowed down with grief. He came to the bed, lifted the cover from the face of his child, gazed at it long and lovingly, and earnestly, murmuring, "My poor boy, he was too good for this earth. God has called him home. I know that he is much better off in heaven, but then we loved him so. It is hard, hard to have him die!"

Keckley, op. cit.

He was his father's favorite. They were intimates—often seen hand in hand.

Keckley, op. cit., account of
Nathaniel Parker Willis.

He was his father over again both in magnetic personality and in all his gifts and tastes.

In "Lincoln's Sons,"
by Ruth Painter Randall.

He was the child in whom Lincoln had invested his fondest hopes; a small mirror of himself, as it were, to whom he could speak frankly, openly, and confidingly.

In "Reckoning: An Insider's Memories of
Difficult Times," by Tyron Philian.

Will was the true picture of Mr. Lincoln, in every way, even to carrying his head slightly inclined toward his left shoulder.

Burlingame, op. cit., account of a
Springfield neighbor.

One feels such love for the little ones, such anticipation that all that is lovely in life will be known by them, such fondness for that set of attributes manifested uniquely in each: mannerisms of bravado, of vulnerability, habits of speech and mispronouncement and so forth; the smell of the hair and head, the feel of the tiny hand in yours—and then the little one is gone! Taken! One is thunderstruck that such a brutal violation has occurred in what had previously seemed a benevolent world. From nothingness, there arose great love; now, its source nullified, that love, searching and sick, converts to the most abysmal suffering imaginable.

In "Essay Upon the Loss of a Child,"
by Mrs. Rose Milland.

"This is the hardest trial of my life," he confessed to the nurse, and in a spirit of rebellion this man, overweighted with care and sorrows, cried out: "Why is it? Why is it?"

In "Abraham Lincoln: The Boy and
the Man," by James Morgan.

Great sobs choked his utterance. He buried his head in his hands, and his tall frame was convulsed with emotion. I stood at the foot of the bed, my eyes full of tears, looking at the man in silent, awe-stricken wonder. His grief unnerved him, and made him a weak, passive child. I did not dream that his rugged nature could be so moved. I shall never forget those solemn moments—genius and greatness weeping over love's lost idol.

Keckley, op. cit.

XVIII.

Willie Lincoln was the most lovable boy I ever knew, bright, sensible, sweet-tempered and gentle-mannered.

In "Tad Lincoln's Father,"
by Julia Taft Bayne.

He was the sort of child people imagine their children will be, before they have children.

Randall, op. cit.

His self-possession—*aplomb,* as the French call it—was extraordinary.

Willis, op. cit.

His mind was active, inquisitive, and conscientious; his disposition was amiable and affectionate; his impulses were kind and generous; and his words and manners were gentle and attractive.

In "Funeral Oration for Willie Lincoln,"
by Phineas D. Gurley, in "Illinois
State Journal."

He never failed to seek me out in the crowd, shake hands, and make some pleasant remark; and this in a boy of ten years of age, was, to say the least, endearing to a stranger.

Willis, op. cit.

Willie had a gray and very baggy suit of clothes, and his style was altogether different from that of the curled darlings of the fashionable mothers.

In "The Truth About Mrs. Lincoln," by Laura Searing (writing as Howard Glyndon).

I was one day passing the White House, when he was outside with a play-fellow on the sidewalk. Mr. Seward drove in, with Prince Napoleon and two of his *suite* in the carriage; and, in a mock-heroic way—terms of intimacy evidently existing between the boy and the Secretary—the official gentleman took off his hat, and the Napoleon did the same, all making the young Prince President a ceremonial salute. Not a bit staggered with the homage, Willie drew himself up to his full height, took off his little cap with graceful self-possession, and bowed down formally to the ground, like a little ambassador.

Willis, op. cit.

There was a glow of intelligence and feeling on his face which made him particularly interesting and caused strangers to speak of him as a fine little fellow.

Searing, op. cit.

It is easy to see how a child, thus endowed, would, in the course of eleven years, entwine himself round the hearts of those who knew him best.

Gurley, op. cit.

A sunny child, dear & direct, abundantly open to the charms of the world.

In "They Knew the Lincoln Boys," by Carol Dreiser, account of Simon Weber.

A sweet little muffin of a fellow, round and pale, a long shock of bangs often falling before his eyes, who would, when he found himself moved or shy, involuntarily perform a rapid opening and closing of the eyes: blink, blink, blink.

In "The President's Little Men,"
by Opal Stragner.

When confronted with some little unfairness, his face would darken with concern, and his eyes well up with tears, as if, in that unfortunate particular, he had intuited the injustice of the larger enterprise. Once a playmate brought along a dead robin he had just killed with a stone, held tong-like between two sticks. Willie spoke brusquely to the boy, seized the bird away, took it off to bury it, was low and quiet for the rest of the day.

In "Lincoln's Lost Angel,"
by Simon Iverness.

His leading trait seemed to be a fearless and kindly frankness, willing that everything should be as different as it pleased, but resting unmoved in his own conscious single-heartedness. I found I was studying him irresistibly, as one of those sweet problems of childhood that the world is blessed with in rare places.

Willis, op. cit.

Privately, after the service, Dr. Gurley told people that shortly before death Willie had asked him to take the six dollars that were his savings out of the bank on his bureau and give them to the missionary society.

Kunhardt and Kunhardt, op. cit.

With all the splendor that was around this little fellow in his new home, he was so bravely and beautifully *himself*—and that only. A wild flower transplanted from the prairie to the hot-house, he retained his prairie habits, unalterably pure and simple, till he died.

Willis, op. cit.

Many months later, going through some old clothing for Mrs. Lincoln, I found, in a coat-pocket, a tiny wadded-up mitten. Many memories came back to me and I burst into tears. I will remember that little boy forever, and his sweet ways.

Hilyard, op. cit., account of
Sophie Lenox, maid.

He was not perfect; he was, remember, a little boy. Could be wild, naughty, overwrought. He was *a boy*. However—it must be said—he was quite a *good* boy.

Hilyard, op. cit., account of
D. Strumphort, butler.

XIX.

About noon, The President, Mrs. Lincoln, & Robert came down and visited the lost and loved one for the last time, together. They desired that there should be no spectator of their last sad moments in that house with their dead child & brother. They remained nearly 1/2 an hour. While they were thus engaged there came one of the heaviest storms of rain & wind that has visited this city for years, and the terrible storm without seemed almost in unison with the storm of grief within.

In "Witness to the Young Republic: A Yankee's Journal, 1828–1870," by Benjamin Brown French, edited by D. B. Cole and J. J. McDonough.

During the half hour the family was closeted with the dead boy, lightning cleaved the dark sky outside, thunder as terrible as artillery fire made the crockery shudder, and violent winds charged in from the northwest.

Epstein, op. cit.

From throughout the spacious halls that evening great sounds of grief could be heard, not all emanating from the direction of the room where Mrs. Lincoln lay insensate; the President's deeper groans could also be heard.

In "My Ten Years at the White House," by Elliot Sternlet.

A century and a half has passed, and yet it still seems intrusive to dwell upon that horrible scene—the shock, the querulous disbelief, the savage cries of sorrow.

Epstein, op. cit.

It was only just at bedtime, when the boy would normally present himself for some talk or roughhousing, that Mr. Lincoln seemed truly mindful of the irreversibility of the loss.

In "Selected Memories from a Life of Service," by Stanley Hohner.

Around midnight I entered to ask if I could bring him something. The sight of him shocked me. His hair was wild, his face pale, with signs of recent tears plainly evident. I marveled at his agitated manner and wondered what might be the outcome if he did not find some relief. I had recently been to visit an iron-works in the state of Pennsylvania, where a steam-release valve had been demonstrated to me; the President's state put me in mind of the necessity of such an apparatus.

Hilyard, op. cit., account of D. Strumphort, butler.

XX.

The unkempt gentleman was fussing over the small form now, stroking the hair, patting and rearranging the pale, doll-like hands.

roger bevins iii

As the lad stood nearby, uttering many urgent entreaties for his father to look *his* way, fuss over and pat *him*.

the reverend everly thomas

Which the gentleman appeared not to hear.

roger bevins iii

Then this already troubling and unseemly display descended to a new level of—

hans vollman

We heard an intake of breath from the Reverend, who, appearance notwithstanding, is not easily shocked.

roger bevins iii

He is going to pick that child up, the Reverend said.

hans vollman

And so he did.

The man lifted the tiny form out of the—

roger bevins iii

Sick-box.

hans vollman

The man bent, lifted the tiny form from the box, and, with surprising grace for one so ill-made, sat all at once on the floor, gathering it into his lap.

roger bevins iii

Sinking his head into the place between chin and neck, the gentleman sobbed, raggedly at first, then unreservedly, giving full vent to his emotions.

the reverend everly thomas

While the lad darted back and forth nearby, in an apparent agony of frustration.

hans vollman

For nearly ten minutes the man held the—

roger bevins iii

Sick-form.

hans vollman

The boy, frustrated at being denied the attention he felt *he* deserved, moved in and leaned against his father, as the father continued to hold and gently rock the—

the reverend everly thomas

Sick-form.

hans vollman

At one point, moved, I turned away from the scene and found we were not alone.

roger bevins iii

A crowd had gathered outside.

the reverend everly thomas

All were silent.

roger bevins iii

As the man continued to gently rock his child.

the reverend everly thomas

While his child, simultaneously, stood quietly leaning against him.

hans vollman

Then the gentleman began to speak.

roger bevins iii

The lad threw one arm familiarly around his father's neck, as he must often have done, and drew himself in closer, until his head was touching his father's head, the better to hear the words the man was whispering into the neck of the—

hans vollman

His frustration then becoming unbearable, the boy began to—

roger bevins iii

The lad began to enter himself.

hans vollman

As it were.

roger bevins iii

The boy began to enter himself; had soon entered himself entirely, and at this, the man began sobbing anew, as if he could feel the altered condition of that which he held.

the reverend everly thomas

It was all too much, too private, and I left that place, and walked alone.

hans vollman

As did I.

roger bevins iii

I lingered there, transfixed, uttering many prayers.

the reverend everly thomas

XXI.

Mouth at the worm's ear, Father said:

We have loved each other well, dear Willie, but now, for reasons we cannot understand, that bond has been broken. But our bond can never be broken. As long as I live, you will always be with me, child.

Then let out a sob

Dear Father crying   That was hard to see   And no matter how I patted & kissed & made to console, it did no

You were a joy, he said. Please know that. Know that you were a joy. To us. Every minute, every season, you were a—you did a good job. A good job of being a pleasure to know.

Saying all this to the worm!   How I wished him to say it to me   And to feel his eyes on me   So I thought, all right, by Jim, I will get him to see me   And in I went   It was no bother at all   Say, it felt all right   Like I somewhat belonged in

In there, held so tight, I was now partly also in Father

And could know exactly what he was

Could feel the way his long legs lay   How it is to have a beard   Taste coffee in the mouth and, though not thinking in words exactly, knew that *the feel of him in my arms has done me good. It has. Is this wrong? Unholy? No, no, he is mine, he is ours, and therefore I must be, in that sense, a god in this; where he is concerned I may decide what is best. And I believe this has done me good. I remember him. Again. Who he was. I had forgotten somewhat already. But here: his exact proportions, his suit smelling of him still, his forelock between my fingers, the heft of him familiar from when he would fall asleep in the parlor and I would carry him up to—*

It has done me good.

I believe it has.

It is secret. A bit of secret weakness, that shores me up; in shoring me up, it makes it more likely that I shall do my duty in other matters; it hastens the end of this period of weakness; it harms no one; therefore, it is not wrong, and I shall take away from here this resolve: I may return as often as I like, telling no one, accepting whatever help it may bring me, until it helps me no more.

Then Father touched his head to mine.

Dear boy, he said, I will come again. That is a promise.

willie lincoln

XXII.

After perhaps thirty minutes the unkempt man left the white stone home and stumbled away into the darkness.

Entering, I found the boy sitting in one corner.

My father, he said.

Yes, I said.

He said he will come again, he said. He promised.

I found myself immeasurably and inexplicably moved.

A miracle, I said.

the reverend everly thomas

XXIII.

At approximately one a.m. tonight per this report Pres Lincoln arrived at front gate requesting he be allowed to enter same accordingly and not knowing what else to do given his position which is President not an inconsiderable position for him to have or anyone I did allow him entry even though as you know Tom protocol states once gate locked is not to be unlocked until such time as unlocking is scheduled to wit morning but since it was Pres himself asking was a bit of a horned dilemma staring in my face and also I was somewhat groggy it being late as mentioned above and having given myself over yesterday to some fun in the park with my own children Philip Mary & Jack Jr. thereby being somewhat tired and I admit dozing a bit at your desk Tom. Did not question Pres as to what was he doing here or something like that only when our eyes met he gave me such a frank friendly somewhat pained look as if to say well friend this is rather odd I know it but with eyes so needful I could not refuse him as his boy is just today interred so you might well imagine how you or I might act or feel in a similar sad spot Tom if yr Mitchell or my Philip Mary or Jack Jr. was to expire well no use thinking of that.

Had no driver with him but had arrived alone on small horse which I was quite surprised at him being Pres and all and say his legs are quite long and his horse quite short so it appeared some sort of man-sized insect had attached itself to that poor unfortunate nag who freed of his burden stood tired and hangdog and panting as if thinking I will have quite the story to tell the other horsies upon my return if they are still awake at which time Pres requested key to Carroll crypt and accordingly I handed it over and watched him wander off across grounds wishing I'd had courtesy at least to offer him loan of lamp which he did not have one but went forth into that stygian dark like pilgrim going forward into a trackless desert Tom it was awful sad.

Tom here is the strange part he has been gone for ever so long. Is still gone as I write. Where is he Tom. Lost is he lost. Lost in there or fell and broke something lying there crying out.

Just now stepped out listened no cries.

Where is he at this time do not know Tom.

Maybe out there in woods somewhere recovering from visit indulging in solitary cry?

In watchman's logbook, 1860–78, Oak Hill Cemetery, entry by Jack Manders, night of February 25, 1862, quoted by arrangement with Mr. Edward Sansibel.

XXIV.

It would be difficult to overstate the vivifying effect this visitation had on our community.

hans vollman

Individuals we had not seen in years walked out, crawled out, stood shyly wringing their hands in delighted incredulity.

the reverend everly thomas

Individuals we had *never* seen before, now made their anxious debuts.

roger bevins iii

Who knew Edenston to be a tiny man in green, wig askew? Who knew Cravwell to be a giraffe-like woman in spectacles, holding a book of light verse she had written?

hans vollman

Flattery, deference, smiles, ringing laughter, affectionate greetings were the order of the day.

roger bevins iii

Men milled about under that high February moon, complimenting each other's suits, enacting familiar gestures: kicking at the dirt, throwing a stone, feigning a punch. Women held hands, faces upturned, calling one another *lovely* and *dear*, pausing beneath trees to exchange strange confidences withheld during many years of seclusion.

the reverend everly thomas

People were *happy,* that was what it was; they had recovered that notion.

hans vollman

It was the idea, the very idea, that someone—

roger bevins iii

From that other place—

hans vollman

That someone from that other place would deign to—

roger bevins iii

It was the *touching* that was unusual.

the reverend everly thomas

It was not unusual for people from that previous place to be *around.*

hans vollman

Oh, they were around often enough.

the reverend everly thomas

With their cigars, wreaths, tears, crepe, heavy carriages, black horses stamping at the gate.

roger bevins iii

Their rumors, their discomfort, their hissing of things having nothing at all to do with us.

the reverend everly thomas

Their warm flesh, steaming breath, moist eyeballs, chafing undergarments.

roger bevins iii

Their terrible shovels laid carelessly against our trees.

the reverend everly thomas

But the *touching.* My God!

hans vollman

Not that they didn't sometimes touch us.

roger bevins iii

Oh, they'd touch you, all right. They'd wrangle you into your sick-box.

hans vollman

Dress you how they wanted you. Stitch and paint you as necessary.

roger bevins iii

But once they had you how they wanted you, they never touched you again.

hans vollman

Well, Ravenden.

the reverend everly thomas

They touched Ravenden again.

roger bevins iii

But that sort of touching—

hans vollman

No one wants that sort of touching.

the reverend everly thomas

The roof of his stone home was leaking. His sick-box had been damaged.

roger bevins iii

They hauled it into the daylight, threw open the lid.

the reverend everly thomas

It was autumn and leaves were falling all over the poor fellow. Proud type, too. Banker. Claimed to have owned a mansion on the—

hans vollman

They yanked him out of the box and dropped him—thump!—into a new one. Then asked, in jest, had it hurt, and, if so, did he wish to file a complaint? Then they enjoyed a lengthy smoke, poor Ravenden (half in and half out, head tilted at a most uncomfortable angle) calling out feebly all the while for them to kindly place him in a less unseemly—

the reverend everly thomas

That kind of touching—

roger bevins iii

No one wants that.

hans vollman

But this—this was different.

roger bevins iii

The holding, the lingering, the kind words whispered directly into the ear? My God! My God!

the reverend everly thomas

To be touched so lovingly, so fondly, as if one were still—

roger bevins iii

Healthy.

hans vollman

As if one were still worthy of affection and respect? It was cheering. It gave us hope.

the reverend everly thomas

We were perhaps not so unlovable as we had come to believe.

roger bevins iii

XXV.

Please do not misunderstand. We had been mothers, fathers. Had been husbands of many years, men of import, who had come here, that first day, accompanied by crowds so vast and sorrowful that, surging forward to hear the oration, they had damaged fences beyond repair. Had been young wives, diverted here during childbirth, our gentle qualities stripped from us by the naked pain of that circumstance, who left behind husbands so enamored of us, so tormented by the horror of those last moments (the notion that we had gone down that awful black hole pain-sundered from ourselves) that they had never loved again. Had been bulky men, quietly content, who, in our first youth, had come to grasp our own unremarkableness and had, cheerfully (as if bemusedly accepting a heavy burden), shifted our life's focus; if we would not be *great*, we would be *useful;* would be rich, and kind, and thereby able to effect good: smiling, hands in pockets, watching the world we had subtly improved walking past (this empty dowry filled; that education secretly funded). Had been affable, joking servants, of whom our masters had grown fond for the cheering words we managed as they launched forth on days full of import. Had been grandmothers, tolerant and frank, recipients of certain dark secrets, who, by the quality of their unjudging listening, granted tacit forgiveness, and thus let in the sun. What I mean to say is, we had been *considerable.* Had been *loved.* Not lonely, not lost, not freakish, but wise, each in his or her own way. Our departures caused pain. Those who had loved us sat upon their beds, heads in hand; lowered their faces to tabletops, making animal noises. We had been loved, I say, and remembering us, even many years later, people would smile, briefly gladdened at the memory.

the reverend everly thomas

And yet.

roger bevins iii

And yet no one had ever come here to hold one of us, while speaking so tenderly.

hans vollman

Ever.

roger bevins iii

XXVI.

Before long a sea of us surrounded the white stone home.

the reverend everly thomas

And pushing forward, pressed the boy for details: How had it felt, being held like that? Had the visitor really promised to come again? Had he offered any hope for the alteration of the boy's fundamental circumstance? If so, might said hope extend to us as well?

roger bevins iii

What did we want? We wanted the lad to *see* us, I think. We wanted his blessing. We wanted to know what this apparently charmed being thought of our particular reasons for remaining.

hans vollman

Truth be told, there was not one among the many here—not even the strongest—who did not entertain some lingering doubt about the wisdom of his or her choice.

roger bevins iii

The loving attentions of the gentleman having improved our notion of the boy, we found ourselves craving the slightest association.

the reverend everly thomas

With this new-established prince.

roger bevins iii

Soon the line of people waiting to speak to the lad ran down the path as far back as the tan sandstone home of Everfield.

hans vollman

XXVII.

I will be brief.

jane ellis

I doubt it.

mrs. abigail blass

Mrs. Blass, please. Everyone will get a—

the reverend everly thomas

"Once at the Christmastide Papa took us to a wonderful village festival." Ugh.

mrs. abigail blass

Please don't crowd. Simply stay in line. All will be accommodated.

hans vollman

She yips and yips and must always be first. In all things. How, please tell me, does she merit such—

mrs. abigail blass

You could learn a thing or two from her, Mrs. Blass. Look at her posture.

hans vollman

How calm she remains.

the reverend everly thomas

How clean her clothing is kept.

roger bevins iii

Gentlemen?

If I may?

Once at the Christmastide Papa took us to a wonderful village festival. Above a meatshop doorway hung a marvelous canopy of carcasses: deer with the entrails pulled up and out and wired to the outside of the bodies like tremendous bright-red garlands; pheasants and drakes hung head-down, wings spread by use of felt-covered wires, the colors of which matched the respective feathers (it was done most skillfully); twin pigs stood on either side of the doorway with game hens mounted upon them like miniature riders. All of it bedraped in greenery and hung with candles. I wore white. I was a beautiful child in white, long rope of hair hanging down my back, and I would willfully swing it, just so. I hated to leave, and threw a tantrum. To assuage me, Papa bought a deer and let me assist him in strapping it to the rear of the carriage. Even now, I can see it: the countryside scrolling out behind us in the near-evening fog, the limp deer dribbling behind its thin blood-trail, stars blinking on, creeks running and popping beneath us as we lurched over groaning bridges of freshcut timber, proceeding homeward through the gathering—

jane ellis

Ugh.

mrs. abigail blass

I felt myself a new species of child. Not a boy (most assuredly) but neither a (mere) girl. That skirt-bound race perpetually moving about serving tea had nothing to do with *me*.

I had such high hopes, you see.

The boundaries of the world seemed vast. I would visit Rome, Paris, Constantinople. Underground cafés presented in my mind where, crushed against wet walls, a (handsome, generous) friend and I sat discussing—many things. Deep things, new ideas. Strange green lights shone in the streets, the sea lapped nearby against greasy tilted moorings; there was trouble afoot, a revolution, into which my friend and I must—

Well, as is often the case, my hopes were . . . not realized. My husband was not handsome and was not generous. He was a bore. Was not rough with me but neither was he tender. We did not go to Rome or Paris or Constantinople, but only back and forth, endlessly, to Fairfax, to visit his aged mother. He did not seem to *see* me, but only endeavored to *possess* me; would wiggle his little roach of a mustache at me whenever he found me (as he so often found me) "silly." I would say something that I felt had truth and value in it, regarding, for example, his failure to get ahead in his profession (he was a complainer, always fancying himself the victim of some conspiracy, who, finding himself thus disrespected, would pick some trivial fight and soon be sacked) but he need only wiggle that mustache and pronounce mine "a woman's view of the thing" and—that was that. I was dismissed. To hear him bragging about the impression he had made on some minor functionary with a "witty" remark, and to have been there, and heard that remark, and noticed the functionary and his wife barely able to refrain from laughing in the face of this pompous little nobody was . . . trying. I had been that beautiful child in white, you see, Constantinople, Paris, and Rome in her heart, who had not known, at that time, that she was of "an inferior species," a "mere" woman. And then, of an evening, to have him shoot me that certain look (I knew it well) that meant "Brace yourself, madam, I will soon be upon you, all hips and tongue, little mustache having seemingly reproduced itself so as to be able to cover every entry point, so to speak, and afterward I will be upon you again, fishing for a compliment" was more than I could bear.

Then the children came.

The children—yes. Three marvelous girls.

In those girls I found my Rome, my Paris, my Constantinople.

He has no interest in them at all, except he likes to use them to prop himself up in public. He disciplines this one too harshly for some minor infraction, dismisses that one's timidly offered opinion, lectures loudly to all regarding some obvious fact ("You see, girls, the moon hangs up there among the stars") as if he has just that instant discovered it—then glances around to judge what effect his manliness is having on passers-by.

jane ellis

If you please.

Many are waiting.

mrs. abigail blass

Is *he* to care for them?

In my absence?

Cathryn is soon to begin school. Who will make sure her clothes are correct? Maribeth has a bad foot and is self-conscious and often comes home in tears. To whom will she cry? Alice is nervous, for she has submitted a poem. It is not a very good poem. I have a plan to give her Shakespeare to read, and Dante, and we will work on some poems together.

They seem especially dear to me now. During this pause. Fortunately, it is a minor surgery only. A rare opportunity, really, for a person to pause and take stock of her—

jane ellis

Mrs. Ellis was a stately, regal woman, always surrounded by three gelatinous orbs floating about her person, each containing a likeness of one of her daughters. At times these orbs grew to extreme size, and would bear down upon her, and crush out her blood and other fluids as she wriggled beneath their terrible weight, refusing to cry out, as this would indicate displeasure, and at other times these orbs departed from her and she was greatly tormented, and must rush about trying to find them, and when she did, would weep in relief, at which time they would once again begin bearing down upon her; but the worst torment of all for Mrs. Ellis was when one of the orbs would establish itself before her eyes exactly life-sized and become completely translucent and she would thus be able to mark the most fine details of the clothing, facial expression, disposition, etc., of the daughter inside, who, in a heartfelt manner, would begin explaining some difficulty into which she had lately been thrust (especially in light of Mrs. Ellis's sudden absence). Mrs. Ellis would show the most acute judgment and abundant love as she explained, in a sympathetic voice, how the afflicted child might best address the situation at hand—but alas (herein lay the torment) the child could not see or hear her in the least, and would work herself, before the eyes of Mrs. Ellis, into ever-increasing paroxysms of despair, as the poor woman began to dash about, trying to evade the orb, which would pursue her with what can only be described as a sadistic intelligence, anticipating her every move, thrusting itself continually before her eyes, which, as far as I could tell, were incapable, at such times, of closing.

the reverend everly thomas

On other days, everyone she met manifested as a giant mustache with legs.

hans vollman

Yes, her way is hard.

roger bevins iii

Not so hard. She's a rich one.
You can tell by her voice.

mrs. abigail blass

Young sir, may I ask—a kindness?

jane ellis

Snooty.

mrs. abigail blass

If you are allowed back to that previous place, will you check Cathryn's clothing and console Maribeth and tell Alice it is not a sin to fail in one's first attempt? Assure them I have been thinking of them since I arrived here and am trying to make my way home, and that even as the ether was administered, I was thinking of them, of them and only—

jane ellis

Take the money, I said. I am calm.

mr. maxwell boise

Again pushed aside?
Because I am small?

mrs. abigail blass

Perhaps it is because you are so dirty.

roger bevins iii

I live close to the ground, sir. As I believe you—

mrs. abigail blass

Your slippers are absolutely black with filth.

roger bevins iii

Take the money, I said. I am calm.

You will also, sir, please, remain calm, I said. We have no enmity between us of which I am aware. Let us regard this as a simple business transaction. I will hand you my wallet, just so, and then, with your permission, be on my—

No, no, no.

No no no.

Entirely the wrong & illogical thing for you to—

Low stars, blurred rooftops.

& I am punc tured.

mr. maxwell boise

Try now, Mrs. Blass.

roger bevins iii

Mrs. Blass, notoriously frugal, filthy, gray-haired, and tiny (smaller than a baby), spent her nights racing about, gnawing at rocks and twigs, gathering these things to her, defending them zealously, passing the long hours counting and recounting these meager possessions.

the reverend everly thomas

The opportunity to finally address the lad, there in front of that festive crowd, struck that diminutive lady with a sudden case of stage-fright.

hans vollman

You have one thousand three hundred dollars in the First Bank, I believe?

the reverend everly thomas

Yes.

Thank you, Reverend.

I have one thousand three hundred dollars in the First Bank. In an upstairs room I will not specify I have four thousand in gold coin. I have two horses and fifteen goats and thirty-one chickens and seventeen dresses, worth, in total, some three thousand, eight hundred dollars. But am a widow. What seems like abundance is in fact scarcity. The tide runs out but never runs in. The stones roll downhill but do not roll back up. Therefore you will understand my reluctance to indulge in wastefulness. I have over four hundred twigs and nearly sixty pebbles of various sizes. I have two dead-bird parts, dirt motes too numerous to count. Before retiring I count my dead-bird parts, twigs, pebbles, and motes, rending each with my teeth to ensure all are still real. Upon waking I often find myself short several items. Proving the presence of thieves and justifying those tendencies for which many here (I know they do) judge me harshly. But they are not old women, menaced by frailty, surrounded by enemies, the tide going only out, out, out . . .

mrs. abigail blass

So many were still waiting A shifting mass of gray and black As far as the eye could People in the moonlight outside pushing and shoving, standing on tip-toe to see

Me

Faces thrusting into the doorway to blurt their sad This or that None were content All had been wronged Neglected Overlooked Misunderstood Many wore the old-time leggings and wigs and

willie lincoln

When in my merry red Jacket of Velvet I moved past Flower-bright Hedges in the full Flush of my Youth, I cut a fine Figure indeed. All who saw, thought well of Me. Men of the Town would Stutter upon my Approach, my SHARDS would step aside, awed, as I Passed.

This is what I should like the young Swain to know.

And many was the time I pounded my Lust out in the Night to good Result; pounding my good Wife or, if she was indisposed, pounding my SHARDS, whom I called SHARDS, for they were, indeed, dark as Night, like unto so many SHARDS of COAL, which did give me abundant Heat. I need only Seize a SHARD-LASS up, & Ignoring the Cries of her SHARD-MAN, would—

lieutenant cecil stone

Good Lord.

hans vollman

He is in fine form tonight.

roger bevins iii

Bear in mind, Lieutenant: he is but a child.

hans vollman

And 'twas a Goodly thing, to so Diminish that SHARD-MAN in the Eyes of the Others, and this Message going 'round, their Behavior was

Improv'd, and the next working Day even the most Behemoth of those SHARDS would lower his Eyes, for it was I who held the WHIP & the PISTOL and each SHARD knew that, were he to Offend me, that Night would be Costly to Him, & my FEE for his Offense would be that one most Dear to him, and I would kick open his Door and drag his LASS out & remove her to my Quarters, and the evening's Entertainment would Commence, and that SHARD would be made to give off SPARKS. Consequently, my Fields were Quiet, and when any Order was given, a Dozen pair of Hands rushed to Fulfill it, even as those yellow Weary eyes glanced up, to see, did I Note it, and would I Excuse them & theirs from my Pleasure.

In this way I converted SHARD to Ally, & made them Foes to one another.

lieutenant cecil stone

During these confident-aggressive episodes, fueled by these boastful assertions, Lieutenant Stone's bodily mass would be swept upward into an elongate, vertical body-*coiffe*. His body-volume remaining constant, this increase in height would render him quite thin, literally pencil-thin in places, tall as the tallest of our pines.

When finished speaking, he would resume his former proportions, becoming again a man of average size, beautifully dressed, but with terrible teeth.

the reverend everly thomas

Young sir, if we may approach? The little lady and me?

eddie baron

Ah, no. No, no. I'm afraid that will not be possible at this—

the reverend everly thomas

F—— that!

betsy baron

Everyone gets a turn! You said!

eddie baron

We was low and fell lower. That's the main thing we want to—

betsy baron

We didn't even bother bringing our nice s—— into that s——hole by the river. After the Swede kicked us out of the place on G.

eddie baron

We couldn't even fit that f——er, that beautiful couch, through the s——y little door of that s——hole by the river.

betsy baron

I do not even consider that s——y little door of that s——hole by the river a door, when I think of that f——ing door we had on G. What a door! The door on that s——hole by the river would have been ashamed to call itself a door if it ever saw that f——ing magnificent door on G.

Still, we had our fun.

eddie baron

By the river.

betsy baron

Everybody soused and throwing each other into the f——ing drink? With lit stogies and all? And Cziesniewski kept trying to pronounce "Potomac"?

eddie baron

Everybody heaving stones at them washerladies?

betsy baron

Remember when what's-his-name Tentini almost drowned? Then, when Colonel B. revived him, first thing Tentini did was ask for his f——ing mug of punch?

eddie baron

Perhaps that is enough, the Reverend said coldly.

roger bevins iii

Remember that time we left little Eddie at the Parade Ground?

betsy baron

After the Polk whatdoyoucallit.

eddie baron

We'd had a few.

betsy baron

Didn't hurt him.

eddie baron

Might've helped him.

betsy baron

Made him tougher.

eddie baron

If a horse steps on you, you do not die.

betsy baron

You might limp a bit.

eddie baron

And after that be scared of horses.

betsy baron

And dogs.

eddie baron

But wandering around in a crowd for five hours? Does not kill you.

betsy baron

What I think? It helps you. Because then you know how to wander around in a crowd for five hours without crying or panicking.

eddie baron

Well, he cried and panicked a little. Once he got home.

betsy baron

Ah, sweet C——, you protect the G———ed little f——ers from everything, next thing they're calling you to the privy to wipe their a——holes.

One thing I'll say for Eddie Jr. and Mary Mag? They always wiped their own a——holes.

eddie baron

And we didn't have no privy.

betsy baron

Just s—— wherever.

eddie baron

Why don't they ever come see us? That's what I want to know. How long we been here? A pretty f——ing long time. And they never once—

betsy baron

F—— them! Those f——ing ingrate snakes have no G———ed right to blame us for a f——ing thing until they walk a f——ing mile in our

G——ed shoes and neither f——ing one of the little s——heads has walked even a s——ing half-mile in our f——ing shoes.

eddie baron

Enough, said the Reverend.

hans vollman

These were the Barons.

roger bevins iii

Drunk and insensate, lying in the road, run over by the same carriage, they had been left to recover from their injuries in an unmarked disreputable common sick-pit just beyond the dreaded iron fence, the only white people therein, thrown in with several members of the dark race, not one among them, pale or dark, with a sick-box in which to properly recover.

hans vollman

It was not quite *comme il faut* that the Barons should presume to speak to the boy.

the reverend everly thomas

Or be on this side of the fence.

hans vollman

It is not about wealth.

the reverend everly thomas

I was not wealthy.

hans vollman

It is about comportment. It is about, let us say, being "wealthy in spirit."

the reverend everly thomas

The Barons, however, came and went as they pleased. The fence not being an impediment to them.

hans vollman

As in that previous place, they remained unconstrained.

the reverend everly thomas

Ha.

roger bevins iii

Ha ha.

hans vollman

The Barons were followed in rapid succession by Mr. Bunting ("I certainly have nothing of which to be ashamed"), Mr. Ellenby ("I came to this here town with seven dolers stitched in of my panse and do not intend to go any damn plase until someone tell me where in Hel is my dolers"), and Mrs. Proper Fessbitt ("I request *one last Hour* during which the *terrible pain* be not Upon me, so that I may bid Farewell to my Dear Ones in a more *Genial* spirit"), who inched up to the doorway frozen in the same crabbed, fetal posture in which she had spent her last bedridden year in that previous place.

roger bevins iii

Dozens more still excitedly waited to speak with the lad, buoyant with new hope.

hans vollman

But alas, it was not to be.

the reverend everly thomas

XXVIII.

Presently we became aware, by way of certain familiar signs, that trouble was brewing.

roger bevins iii

It happened as it always happens.

the reverend everly thomas

A hush fell across the premises.

roger bevins iii

The scraping of winter branches against winter branches could be heard.

hans vollman

A warm breeze arose, fragrant with all manner of things that give comfort: grass, sun, beer, bread, quilts, cream—this list being different for each of us, each being differently comforted.

roger bevins iii

Flowers of extraordinary color, size, shape, and fragrance sprang forth fully formed from the earth.

the reverend everly thomas

The gray February trees began to blossom.

hans vollman

Then yielded fruit.

the reverend everly thomas

Fruit responsive to one's wishing: only let the mind drift in the direction of a certain color (silver, say) and shape (star) and, of the instant, a bounty of star-shaped silver fruits would sag the limbs of a tree that seconds before had stood fruitless and winter-dead.

roger bevins iii

The paths between our mounds, the spaces beneath trees, the seats of the benches, the crooks and limbs of the trees themselves (in short, every available inch of space) became spontaneously filled, then overfilled, with food of every variety: in pots and upon fine plates; on spits run between boughs; in golden troughs; in diamond tureens; in tiny emerald saucebowls.

the reverend everly thomas

A wall of water rushed in from the north, then divided itself with military precision into dozens of sub-streams, such that each stone home and sick-mound soon had its own dedicated tributary; the water in these tributaries then rather flamboyantly converting itself into coffee, wine, whiskey, and back into water again.

hans vollman

All of these things, we knew (the fruited trees, the sweet breeze, the endless food, the magical streams), comprised merely the advance guard, so to speak, of what was coming.

the reverend everly thomas

Of who was coming.

hans vollman

Sent by them to exert a softening effect.

the reverend everly thomas

We steeled ourselves accordingly.

hans vollman

It was best to roll into a ball, cover the ears, close the eyes, mash the face into the earth, thereby plugging the nose.

roger bevins iii

Strength now, all! shouted Mr. Vollman.

the reverend everly thomas

And they were upon us.

hans vollman

XXIX.

They entered in lengthy procession.

hans vollman

Each of us apprehending them in a different guise.

the reverend everly thomas

Young girls in summer dresses, brown-skinned and jolly, hair unbound, weaving strands of grass into bracelets, giggling as they passed: country girls, joyful and gay.

Like me.

Like I had been.

mrs. abigail blass

A swarm of beautiful young brides arrayed in thinnish things, silk collars fluttering.

hans vollman

Angels, attentive to strangely corporeal wings, one large wing per woman, that, upon retraction, became a pale flag, tightly furled, running down the spine.

the reverend everly thomas

Hundreds of exact copies of Gilbert, my first (my only!) lover. As he had looked on our best afternoon in the carriage house, gray horse-towel wrapped carelessly about his waist.

roger bevins iii

My girls. Cathryn, Maribeth, Alice. Multiple duplicates of each, going along hand in hand, hair up in Trenton braids, each wearing her last-Easter dress and holding a single sunflower.

jane ellis

A greeting Party of SHARD-lasses (Arrayed in the crude Smocks they Favor'd, falling off their Shoulders in deliberate Sluttiness) didst come forth to Grovel before me; but I had seen and Defeated their Ilk many times Before, & did now leave a generous Brown Turd for their Gift, and Retreated me Home, to await their Departure.

lieutenant cecil stone

The brides moved stealthily, like hunters, seeking for any sign of weakness.

hans vollman

Where is my dear Reverend? the lead angel called, her voice redolent of the fragile glass bells we had always rung upon Easter Sunday.

the reverend everly thomas

One of the multiple Gilberts came over and, kneeling beside me, asked, would I kindly unstop my ears and just please *look* at him?

Something in his voice made it impossible to disobey.

He was beautiful beyond measure.

Come with us, he whispered. Here it is all savagery and delusion. You are of finer stuff. Come with us, all is forgiven.

We know what you did, said a second Gilbert. It is all right.

I did not do it, I said. It is not complete.

It is, the first Gilbert said.

I may yet reverse it, I said.

Dear boy, said the second.

Soften, soften, said a third.

You are a wave that has crashed upon the shore, said a fourth.

Kindly don't bother, I said. I have heard all of this—

Let me tell you something, said the second Gilbert harshly. You are not lying on any floor, in any kitchen. Are you? Look around, fool. You delude yourself. It is complete. You have completed it.

We say these things to speed you along, said the first.

roger bevins iii

One of the country girls was Miranda Debb! Sitting there real as dirt beside me, as of yore, legs crossed under the faded yellow skirt she used to favor. Only she seemed so big now, compared to me, like a regular giant!

You are in a tough spot, sweet Abigail, aren't you? she said. Often, upon waking, you find yourself short several items, don't you? Come on, come with us, we're here to set you free. Look at our arms, our legs, our smiles. Are we liars? Who look so healthy? And who've known you so long? Do you remember hiding of a summer day in the hayrick? Your mother calling for you? Digging in then, delighted to be hiding?

It is that times one million where we will take you, said another, who I now recognized as none other than my dear bridesmaid Cynthia Hoynton!

mrs. abigail blass

Eddie, ain't that f——ing Queenie? my Betsy says to me.

And sure enough it was! Queenie being one of the sluts from Perdy's. Who'd give you a good frontal benddown.

Maybe it's time to give it up, skipper, Queenie said.

In a pig's a——, I said.

Eddie, said Betsy.

F—— off, I said. I know what I'm about.

What *are* you about? Queenie said.

To H—— with you, I said.

I believe your wife may feel differently, she said.

She don't, I said. F—— off. We travel together.

I wonder, she said.

Betsy's eyes were cast down.

Good girl, I said. Keep 'em down. Then she can't f——ing f—— with you.

We aren't here to f—— with anyone, Queenie said.

Do the benddown, I said.

Anytime you want us, she said to Betsy. Call out.

Off you go, I said. C——teaser.

eddie baron

At one moment, the angels stepping *en masse* back into a ray of moonlight to impress me with their collective radiance, I glanced up and saw, spread out around the white stone home, a remarkable tableau of suffering: dozens of us, frozen in misery: cowed, prone, crawling, wincing before the travails of the particularized onslaught each was undergoing.

the reverend everly thomas

Abbie, dear, said Miranda Debb, allow me to show you something.

And put her hands on either side of my face.

And I saw! Where they wanted to take me, the tide would run in, and never out. I would live atop a hill and the stones *would* roll up. When they got to me, they would split open. Inside each was a pill. When I took the pill, I had—oh, Glory! All I needed.

For once.

For once in my life.

Miranda dropped her hands from my face and I was just back *here* again.

Did you like that? Miranda said.

Very much, I said.

Come with us then, said her friend, who I saw was good old Susanna Briggs (!), binding her hair up in a cloth, long grass-blade in her mouth.

Two others were playing tag in a gully. Was it Adela and Eva McBain? It was! Some cows were gazing at the tag-game with love. It felt funny that cows could love but that was just the kind of world it was with these sweet girls around!

I can't believe you are a old widow, said Miranda Debb.

And so little, said Susanna Briggs.

You who was always so pretty, said Miranda Debb.

You had it rough, said Cynthia Hoynton.

The tide ran out but never ran in, said Susanna Briggs.

The stones rolled downhill but never rolled back up, said Cynthia Hoynton.

You never in your life was given enough, said Miranda Debb.

My eyes teared up.

That is so true, I said.

You are a wave that has crashed upon the shore, said Miranda.

We say these things to speed you along, said Susanna.

I said I didn't know about any of that but sure would fancy another of those pills.

Come with us then, Miranda said.

The McBains in the gully paused to listen. As did the cows. As did, somehow, the barn.

I was so tired and had been tired for ever so long.

I believe I will come with, I said.

mrs. abigail blass

From off to my left came a shout—of terror or victory, I could not be sure—followed by the familiar, yet always bone-chilling, firesound associated with the matterlightblooming phenomenon.

Who had gone?

I could not tell.

And was still too under siege myself to care.

hans vollman

As if stimulated by this victory, our tormentors now redoubled their efforts.

the reverend everly thomas

Rose petals rained down, a joyful provocation: red, pink, yellow, white, purple. Then translucent petals; striped petals; dotted petals; petals inscribed (when you took one from the ground and looked closely at it) with detailed images (down to the broken flower-stems and dropped toys) of one's childhood yard. Finally golden petals rained down (of real gold!), ticking with each impact against tree or markerstone.

roger bevins iii

Then: singing. Beautiful singing, filled with longing, promise, reassurance, patience, deep fellow-feeling.

hans vollman

It affected one deeply.

the reverend everly thomas

You wanted to f——ing dance.

betsy baron

But you also wanted to f——ing cry.

eddie baron

While dancing.

betsy baron

Mother came   About ten of her   But none smelled the least like Mother   Say, what is that trick   To send a lonesome fellow ten false mothers

Come with us, Willie, one Mother said

But then   All of a sudden   They did smell right   Very right   And cuddled in around me smelling right

Mother   My goodness   Good old

You are a wave that has crashed upon the shore, said a second Mother

Dear Willie, said a third

Dear dear Willie, said a fourth

And all of those Mothers loved me so and wanted me to go with and said they would take me home soon as I was ready.

willie lincoln

When will you know the full pleasures of the marriage-bed; when behold Anna's naked form; when will she turn to you in that certain state, mouth hungry, cheeks flushed; when will her hair, loosened in a wanton gesture, fall at last around you? (Thus spoke Elsbeth Grove, my wife's cousin—or, rather, spoke a deceiving creature fashioned into the exact image of Elsbeth—in a thinnish thing, silk collar fluttering.)

I'll tell you when, said a second bride, whom I now recognized as my own dear grandmother (also arrayed, disconcertingly, in a thinnish thing, collar fluttering). Never. That's finished now. You delude yourself, Kugel.

Since their last visit they had somehow acquired my nickname.

It troubles Anna that you remain here, Elsbeth said. She asked me to relay this message.

I was weakening with every second and knew I must rally some defense.

Is she there now? I said. Waiting for me? In that place to which you so eloquently urge me to go?

I had them now, for though they are happy enough to deceive, they prefer not to lie.

Elsbeth, blushing, cast an anxious glance at Grandmother.

It is—it is rather difficult to answer your question, Elsbeth said.

You are demons, I said. Who assume these familiar forms to lure me thither.

My, but you are honest, Kugel! said Grandmother.

Are you so honest regarding your own situation? said Elsbeth.

Are you "sick," Kugel? said Grandmother. Do doctors put sick people into "sick-boxes"?

I do not recall that practice ever being followed in our time, Elsbeth said.

Therefore what must we conclude, Kugel? said Grandmother. What are you? Where are you? Admit it, dearest, believe it, say it aloud, profit by it, join us.

We say these things to speed you along, said Elsbeth.

And I saw that I must apply the ultimate antidote.

To whom do you speak? I said. Who is hearing you? To whom do you listen? Whose hand do you now follow, as it lifts to point to the heavens? What is the source of the voice causing those looks of consternation to appear even now upon your faces? Here I am. I am here. Am I not?

This had its usual effect.

Confused and deflated, the brides huddled, whispering to one another, devising a new plan of attack.

Fortunately, at that moment, their fraudulent conference was disrupted by the sound of two more distinct and separate firesound/matterlightblooming occurrences: one from the south, one from the northwest.

hans vollman

Eddie took off running at them sounds.

Sometimes he gets pretty f——ing scared of s——.

One of them sluts came right up to me. Then I seen it is not a slut. But our own daughter, Mary Mag! All f——ing dressed up! Finally come to visit! After all these f——ing years of not!

Mother, she said. We are sorry to have been so remiss. Everett and I.

Who's Everett? I said.

Your son, she said. My brother.

Edward, you mean? I said. Eddie? Eddie Jr.?

Edward, yes, correct, sorry, she said. Anyway, we should have come a long time ago. But I have been quite busy. Being successful. And loved. And producing many children of surpassing beauty. And intelligence. As has Everett.

Edward, I said.

Edward, yes, she said. I am just so exhausted! From . . . from all my successes!

Well, that's all right, I said. You're here now, kid.

And Mother? she said. Please know. Everything is all right. You did the best you could. We blame you for nothing. Although we know that you feel you may have, at times, exhibited certain defects of maternal—

I was kind of a s—— mother, wasn't I? I said.

Whatever failures you feel you may have been responsible for, leave them behind you now, she said. All turned out beautifully. Come with us.

Come where though? I said. I don't—

You are a wave that has crashed upon the shore, she said.

See, I don't get that, I said.

Just then Eddie came racing back.

My hero!

Ha.

Clear the f—— out of here, you, he said.

It's Mary Mag, I said.

No it ain't, he said. Watch this.

He picked up a stone and shagged it. Right at Mary Mag! As the stone passed through, she was not Mary Mag anymore at all, but I don't f——ing know who. Or what. Some blob or blast of sun in the shape of a G———n dress!

You, sir, are a fool, the light-blob said.

Then it turned to me.

You, madam, it said. Are less so.

betsy baron

The lead angel took my face into her hands as her wing swished back and forth, putting me in mind of a horse's tail as that animal feeds.

Are you thriving here, Reverend? she said, wing extended lazily above her. Is He whom you served in life present here?

I—I believe He is, I said.

He is, of course, everywhere, she said. But does not like to see you lingering here. Among such low companions.

Her beauty was considerable and increasing by the second. I saw I must end our interview or risk disaster.

Please go, I said. I do not—I do not require you today.

But soon, I think? she said.

Her beauty swelled beyond description.

And I burst into tears.

the reverend everly thomas

As abruptly as it had begun, the onslaught now ended.

hans vollman

As if upon some common signal, our tormentors departed, their song turning somber and mournful.

the reverend everly thomas

The trees went gray in their wake, the food vanished, the streams receded, the breeze fell, the singing ceased.

roger bevins iii

And we were alone.

hans vollman

And all was dismal again.

the reverend everly thomas

XXX.

Mr. Vollman, Reverend Thomas, and I went forth immediately to determine who had succumbed.

roger bevins iii

The first had been the frugal Mrs. Blass.

the reverend everly thomas

Scattered around the surface of her home-place were her treasured dead-bird parts, twigs, motes, et al., now unattended: objects of value no more.

hans vollman

A. G. Coombs, it appeared, had been the second to succumb.

the reverend everly thomas

Poor fellow. None of us knew him well. He had been here many years. But only rarely left his sick-box.

hans vollman

And when he did, was always heard to bark, "Do you know who I am, sir? They hold me a table at Binlay's! I wear the Legion of the Eagle!" I still recall his shock when I told him I did not know of that place. "Binlay's is the finest house of the City!" he exclaimed. "Of what city?" I inquired, and he said Washington, and described the location of that place, but I knew that intersection, and it was, most decidedly, a place of stables, and I told him so. "I pity you!" he said.

But I had shaken him. He sat awhile on his mound, pensively stroking his beard. "But surely you know the esteemed Mr. Humphries?" he thundered.

And now he was gone.

Goodbye, Mr. Coombs, and may they know of Binlay's wherever you are bound!

roger bevins iii

We wandered past many sitting dejectedly upon their mounds or the steps of their stone homes, weeping with the effort of resistance. Others sat quietly sorting through the various seductive visions and temptations to which they had lately been exposed.

the reverend everly thomas

I felt a renewed affection for all who remained.

roger bevins iii

Wheat had been separated from chaff.

the reverend everly thomas

Our path is not for everyone. Many people—I do not mean to disparage them? Lack the necessary resolve.

hans vollman

Nothing matters *sufficiently* to them, that is the thing.

roger bevins iii

Unsure of who the third victim had been, we suddenly remembered the lad.

hans vollman

It seemed unlikely that one so young could have survived such a merciless assault.

the reverend everly thomas

This being the desired outcome—

roger bevins iii

Given his youth—

hans vollman

The alternative being his eternal enslavement—

roger bevins iii

We found ourselves in a saddened but relieved state of mind as we set off to confirm his departure.

the reverend everly thomas

XXXI.

Imagine our surprise when we found him sitting cross-legged on the roof of the white stone home.

hans vollman

Still here, Mr. Vollman said in amazement.

Yes, the lad answered dryly.

roger bevins iii

His appearance was startling.

the reverend everly thomas

The effort of resistance had cost him dearly.

hans vollman

These young ones are not meant to tarry.

the reverend everly thomas

He was out of breath; his hands were shaking; he had lost, by my estimation, approximately half his bodyweight. His cheekbones protruded; his shirt collar hung huge about his suddenly sticklike neck; charcoal-dark rings had appeared under his eyes; all of these combining to give him a peculiar, wraith-like appearance.

roger bevins iii

He had been a chubby boy.

hans vollman

But was chubby no longer.

roger bevins iii

Good God, Mr. Bevins whispered.

hans vollman

It had taken the Traynor girl nearly a month to descend to this level.

roger bevins iii

The fact that you are still here is impressive, the Reverend said to the lad.

Heroic, even, I added.

But ill-advised, said the Reverend.

hans vollman

It is all right, Mr. Vollman said gently. Really it is. We are here. Proceed in peace: you have provided us ample hope, that will last us many years, and do us much good. We thank you, we wish you well, we bless your departure.

the reverend everly thomas

Yes, only I am not going, the boy said.

roger bevins iii

At this the Reverend's face registered a degree of surprise even more pronounced than the usual considerable level of surprise recorded there.

hans vollman

Father promised, the boy said. How would that be, if he came back and found me gone?

Your father is not coming back, said Mr. Vollman.

No time soon, anyway, I said.

At which point you will be in no condition to receive him, said Mr. Vollman.

If your father comes, the Reverend said, we will tell him you had to leave. Explain to him that it was for the best.

You lie, the boy said.

It appeared the boy's degradation had now begun to affect his disposition.

I beg your pardon? said the Reverend.

You three have lied to me from the first, the boy said. Said I should go. What if I had? I would have missed Father entirely. And now you say you will give him a message?

We will, the Reverend said. We most certainly—

But *how* will you? the boy said. Have you a method? Of communication? I did not. When I was there within him.

roger bevins iii

We do, said Mr. Vollman. We do have such a method.

the reverend everly thomas

(Nebulous.
Far from established.)

roger bevins iii

(There has historically been some confusion around this issue.)

hans vollman

Just then, from across the premises, came the sound of Mrs. Delaney, calling out for Mr. Delaney.

the reverend everly thomas

Many years ago, her husband had preceded her to this place. But was no longer here. That is to say, though his sick-form lay just where she had put it, Mr. Delaney himself—

roger bevins iii

Was elsewhere.

the reverend everly thomas

Had gone on.

hans vollman

However, poor Mrs. Delaney could not resolve to follow.

roger bevins iii

Because of some funny business. That had taken place with another Mr. Delaney.

the reverend everly thomas

The brother of her husband.

hans vollman

It had not felt "funny" at the time, but urgent, fated, and wonderful.

roger bevins iii

But now she was of a divided heart: having spent many years in that previous place, longing for this other Delaney, miserably trapped in her marriage—

the reverend everly thomas

She had, within a month of her husband having come here, taken up with that other Delaney, only to find him at once falling in her estimation, because of the reckless disregard he had shown for her husband's (his brother's) memory, this revealing to her that he was of a decayed and avaricious moral character (unlike her husband, who had been, she now saw, upstanding in every way).

hans vollman

Albeit rather literal, and timid, and not nearly the imposing and alluring physical specimen that he, the (morally suspect) brother, was.

roger bevins iii

So she found herself stuck.

hans vollman

Physically longing for *that* Delaney (still back *there*, in that previous place).

the reverend everly thomas

But also desiring to *go*, and see her husband again, and apologize.

roger bevins iii

For having wasted the many years of their life together craving another man.

hans vollman

In short, she did not know whether she was coming or going.

the reverend everly thomas

Going or waiting.

roger bevins iii

So just wandered around, shouting, "Mr. Delaney!"

the reverend everly thomas

Continuously.

hans vollman

We never knew which Delaney she was calling for.

roger bevins iii

Nor did she.

the reverend everly thomas

I say, the lad suddenly gasped, an unmistakable quaver of fear in his voice.

hans vollman

Looking over, my heart sank.

The roof around him had liquefied, and he appeared to be sitting in a gray-white puddle.

roger bevins iii

From out of the puddle, a vine-like tendril emerged.

the reverend everly thomas

Thickening as it approached the boy, it flowed, cobra-like, over the juncture at which his calves crossed.

roger bevins iii

Reaching to brush it away, I found it stiff, more stone than snake.

the reverend everly thomas

A chilling development.

roger bevins iii

The beginning of the end.

hans vollman

XXXII.

If Miss Traynor's case was any indication, this tendril would soon be followed by a succession of others, until the boy was fully secured (Gulliver-like) to the roof.

roger bevins iii

Once secured, he would be rapidly overgrown by what might best be described as a *placental sheen.*

the reverend everly thomas

This sheen then hardening into a shell-like carapace, that carapace would begin to transition through a series of others (*viz.*, the fallen bridge, vulture, dog, terrible hag, etc.), each more detailed and hideous than the last, this process only serving to increase the speed of his downward spiral: the more perverse the carapace, the less "light" (happiness, honesty, positive aspiration) would get in.

roger bevins iii

Driving him ever further from the light.

hans vollman

These memories of Miss Traynor depressed us.

the reverend everly thomas

Bringing to our minds, as they did, the shame of that long-ago night.

roger bevins iii

On which we had abandoned her.

hans vollman

Stumbling away, heads lowered.

roger bevins iii

Tacitly assenting to her doom.

the reverend everly thomas

As she descended.

hans vollman

We remembered her singing merrily all through the initial carapacing, as if to deny what was happening.

roger bevins iii

"A Heavy Bough Hung Down."

hans vollman

Dear child.

the reverend everly thomas

Lovely voice.

hans vollman

Which became steadily less lovely as the initial carapace formed and she took on the form of a girl-sized crow.

roger bevins iii

Cawing out a nightmarish version of that tune.

hans vollman

Flailing at us whenever we drew too near, with one human arm and that tremendous black wing.

the reverend everly thomas

We had not done enough.

hans vollman

Being rather newly arrived back then.

roger bevins iii

And much preoccupied with the challenges of staying.

hans vollman

Which were not inconsiderable.

roger bevins iii

And have not lessened in the meantime.

the reverend everly thomas

My opinion of myself fell somewhat on that occasion.

hans vollman

Yes.

roger bevins iii

The chapel bell now tolled three.

hans vollman

Jolting us back to the present, producing its usual strange, discordant aftertone.

the reverend everly thomas

Selfish, selfish, selfish.

roger bevins iii

The chief two of Mr. Bevins's eyes widened, as if to say: Gentlemen, it is time to go.

the reverend everly thomas

And yet we lingered.
Brushing away such tendrils as appeared.

roger bevins iii

The lad had fallen silent.

hans vollman

Turned inward.

the reverend everly thomas

Fading in and out of consciousness.

hans vollman

Mumbling and tossing, apparently lost in some delirious dream.

roger bevins iii

Mother, he whispered.

the reverend everly thomas

XXXIII.

Mother says I may taste of the candy city   Once I am up and about   She has saved me a chocolate fish and a bee of honey   Says I will someday command a regiment   Live in a grand old house   Marry some sweet & pretty thing   Have little ones of my own   Ha ha   I like that   All of us will meet in my grand old house and have a fine   I will make the jolliest old lady, Mother says   You boys will bring me cakes   Round the clock   While I just sit   How fat I will be   You boys must buy a cart and take turns wheeling me around ha ha

Mother has such a nice way of laughing

We are on the third stairstep   Stairstep Number 3   That has three white roses on it   Here is how it goes from Stairstep Number 1 to Stairstep Number 5 in number of white roses: 2, 3, 5, 2, 6

Mother comes in close   Touches her nose to mine   This is called "nee-nee"   Which I find babyish   But still I allow it from time to

Father comes along, says, Say, can I get in on this pile-up

He can

If Father puts his knees on Stairstep Number 2 and stretches he can reach with his fingers to Stairstep Number 12   He is that long   Has done it   Many times

No more pile-ups   Unless I am strong

Therefore I know what I must   Must stay   Is not easy   But I know honor   Fix bayonets   How to be brave   Is not easy   Remember Col. Ellis   Killed by Rebs   For bravely tearing down the Reb flag from a private   I must stay   If I wish to get   Home   When will I   When may I

Never if weak
Maybe if strong.

willie lincoln

XXXIV.

The boy's eyes flew open.

roger bevins iii

Strange here, he said.
Not strange, said Mr. Bevins. Not really.
One gets used to it, said the Reverend.
If one belongs here, said Mr. Bevins.
Which you don't, said the Reverend.

hans vollman

Just then three gelatinous orbs floated past, as if seeking someone.

the reverend everly thomas

And we realized that Mrs. Ellis had been the third of us to succumb.

roger bevins iii

The orbs were now empty; i.e., contained no daughters.

hans vollman

They paraded sourly by, seemed to glare at us, drifted away down the steep incline to the creek, became dimmer, finally vanished entirely.

the reverend everly thomas

Not strange at all, said Mr. Bevins, blushing slightly.

hans vollman

XXXV.

And there came down upon us a rain of hats.

the reverend everly thomas

Of all types.

roger bevins iii

Hats, laughter, crude jests, the sound of fart-noises made by mouths, from on high: these were the harbingers of the approach of the Three Bachelors.

the reverend everly thomas

Though only they among us could fly, we did not envy them.

hans vollman

Having never loved or been loved in that previous place, they were frozen here in a youthful state of perpetual emotional vacuity; interested only in freedom, profligacy, and high-jinks, railing against any limitation or commitment whatsoever.

the reverend everly thomas

Were all for fun and jollity; distrusted anything serious; lived only for their rollicks.

roger bevins iii

Their boisterous cries often resounding above our premises.

the reverend everly thomas

Some days it was just a steady rain of hats.

roger bevins iii

Of all types.

hans vollman

Of which they seemed to have an inexhaustible supply.

roger bevins iii

A derby, a tinsel-edged cocked, four nice feathered Scotch-caps dropped now in rapid succession, followed by the Bachelors themselves, who touched down gallantly on the roof of the white stone home, each tipping his own hat or cap as he did so.

By your leave, said Mr. Lippert. We seek a Respite.

Flying tires us, said Mr. Kane.

Though we love it, said Mr. Fuller.

Ye Gods, said Mr. Kane, catching sight of the boy.

He don't look so pert, said Mr. Fuller.

I have been somewhat ill, the lad said, rousing himself.

I should say so, said Mr. Kane.

'Tis a bit ripe in this country, said Mr. Fuller, pinching his nose closed.

My father was here and has promised to return, the boy said. I am trying to last.

All best Wishes with that, said Mr. Lippert, raising an eyebrow.

Mind your leg there, kiddo, said Mr. Kane.

Distracted by our guests, we had been remiss: the boy's left leg was now webbed to the roof by several stout new tendrils, each the width of a wrist.

Goodness, the boy said, blushing.

The labor required to get him free was not insignificant, roughly equivalent to that required to uproot a tangle of blackberry roots. He bore the considerable discomfort of that procedure with a soldierly fixity of mind for one so young, letting out only a stoic grunt at each tug, and then, exhausted, fell back into that earlier state of disassociated torpor.

This father of his, said Mr. Fuller in an undertone. Long-legged fellow?

Somewhat dolorous in aspect? said Mr. Lippert.

Tall, a bit raggedy-seeming? said Mr. Kane.

Yes, I said.

Just passed him, said Mr. Fuller.

I beg your pardon? I said.

Just passed him, said Mr. Kane.

Here? Mr. Vollman said incredulously. Still here?

Out near Bellingwether, *Husband, Father, Shipwright,* said Mr. Lippert.

Sitting all quiet-like, said Mr. Fuller.

Just passed him, said Mr. Kane.

the reverend everly thomas

Toodle-oo, said Mr. Fuller.

You will Excuse us, said Mr. Lippert. This is the time of night when we must rapidly Circumnavigate the entire Premises, hovering only inches away from that Dread fence, to see which of us may come the Closest, even while experiencing those nauseating Effects convey'd via Proximity to same.

hans vollman

And off they went, emitting a perfect major triad via fart-noises with their mouths, sending down, as if in farewell, a rain of celebratory hats: flared Tops, Turkish house caps; kepis of various colors; a flower-bedecked Straw, falling rather more slowly than the rest, a lovely thing, redolent of summer.

roger bevins iii

This revelation left us dumbstruck.

hans vollman

Strange that the gentleman had come here in the first place; stranger still that he lingered.

the reverend everly thomas

The Bachelors were not entirely trustworthy.

hans vollman

Terrified of boredom, they were prone to pranks.

roger bevins iii

Had once convinced Mrs. Tessenbaum she was manifesting in lingerie.

hans vollman

After which she spent several years cowering behind a tree.

roger bevins iii

Occasionally hid tiny Mrs. Blass's dead-bird parts, twigs, pebbles, and motes.

the reverend everly thomas

Causing her to race frantically about the premises while they hovered above, encouraging her, with false suggestions, to leap over fallen branches and cross narrow rivulets, which did not seem narrow to her, poor thing, but like great rushing streams.

roger bevins iii

Any assertion by the Bachelors must therefore be regarded with suspicion.

hans vollman

Still, this was intriguing.

roger bevins iii

Merited further investigation.

hans vollman

I think not, the Reverend said sharply, as if intuiting our intention.

Then indicated, with a meaning glance, that he wished a confidential word.

roger bevins iii

XXXVI.

We three sank through the roof, into the white stone home.

hans vollman

It was several degrees cooler there, and smelled of old leaves and mold.

roger bevins iii

And of the gentleman, slightly.

hans vollman

We are here by grace, the Reverend said. Our ability to abide far from assured. Therefore, we must conserve our strength, restricting our activities to only those which directly serve our central purpose. We would not wish, through profligate activity, to appear ungrateful for the mysterious blessing of our continued abiding. For we are here, but for how long, or by what special dispensation, it is not ours to—

roger bevins iii

Several of Mr. Bevins's many eyes, I noted, were rolling.

hans vollman

Waiting for the Reverend to dismount from his high horse, Mr. Vollman was amusing himself by repeatedly placing a pebble on his tremendous member and watching it tumble down.

roger bevins iii

We must look out for ourselves, the Reverend said. And, by doing so, we protect the boy as well. He must hear nothing of this rumor, which would only serve to raise his hopes. As we know, only utter hopelessness will lead him to do what he must. Therefore, not a word. Are we in agreement?

We mumbled our assent.

hans vollman

Lacking the necessary spring in his (ancient) legs (he had come here already quite old), the Reverend began clawing his way up one wall and soon (although not *that* soon) vanished through the ceiling.

roger bevins iii

Leaving Mr. Bevins and me there below, alone.

hans vollman

In truth, we were bored, so very bored, so continually bored.

roger bevins iii

Each night passed with a devastating sameness.

hans vollman

We had sat every branch on every tree. Had read and re-read every stone. Had walked down (run down, crawled down, laid upon) every walk, path, and weedy trail, had waded every brook; possessed a comprehensive knowledge of the textures and tastes of the four distinct soil types here; had made a thorough inventory of every hair-style, costume, hair-pin, watch-fob, sock-brace, and belt worn by our compatriots; I had heard Mr. Vollman's story many thousands of times, and had, I fear, told him my own at least as many times.

roger bevins iii

In short, it was dull here, and we craved the slightest variation.

hans vollman

Anything new was a treasure; we longed for any adventure, the merest lark.

roger bevins iii

There would be no harm, we thought, in taking a quick trip.

hans vollman

Out to where the gentleman sat.

roger bevins iii

We need not even tell the Reverend we were going.
We could just . . . go.

hans vollman

It was always a relief to be free of the old bore for a bit.

roger bevins iii

XXXVII.

Bursting out through the front wall, Mr. Bevins and I set off.

hans vollman

Ignoring the Reverend's peevish cries of protest from the roof.

roger bevins iii

Cutting down through the clover-engorged dell occupied by the seven flood-sickened members of the Palmer family, we shortly reached that thin gray-slate trail that runs below, passing between Coates on one side and Wemberg on the other.

hans vollman

Wended our way past Federly, *Blessed are those who die in the Light*.

roger bevins iii

A chess-piece-looking monument, topped with a vase, that ends in what looks like a nipple.

hans vollman

And proceeded through the M. Boyden/G. Boyden/Gray/Hebbard cluster.

roger bevins iii

Into that slight hollow which is, in spring, overgrown with foxglove and coneflower.

hans vollman

But was now a massive dormant tangle of gray.

roger bevins iii

Wherein two slothful winter birds glared at us as we passed.

hans vollman

Birds being distrustful of our ilk.

roger bevins iii

Jogging down the far side of the North Hill, we greeted Merkel (kicked by a bull but still looking forward to the dance); Posterbell (a dandy whose looks had gone, who fervently wished that his hair might be restored and his gums might reverse their recession and the muscles of his arms might no longer resemble flaccid straps and his dinner suit be brought to him, and a bottle of scent and a bouquet of flowers, so that he might once again go courting); Mr. and Mrs. West (fire with no possible cause, as they were always meticulously careful regarding management of the hearth); and Mr. Dill (mumbling contentedly about his grandson's excellent university marks, eagerly anticipating the spring graduation).

hans vollman

And proceeded past Trevor Williams, former hunter, seated before the tremendous heap of all the animals he had dispatched in his time: hundreds of deer, thirty-two black bear, three bear cubs, innumerable coons, lynx, foxes, mink, chipmunks, wild turkeys, woodchucks, and cougars; scores of mice and rats, a positive tumble of snakes, hundreds of cows and calves, one pony (carriage-struck), twenty thousand or so insects, each of which he must briefly hold, with loving attention, for a period ranging from several hours to several months, depending on the quality of loving attention he could muster and the state of fear the beast happened to have been in at the time of its passing. Being thus held (the product of time and loving attention being found sufficient, that is), that particular creature would heave up, then trot or fly or squirm away, diminishing Mr. Williams's heap by one.

roger bevins iii

It was an extraordinary pile, nearly as tall as the chapel spire.

hans vollman

He had been a prodigious hunter and had many years of hard work yet ahead of him.

roger bevins iii

He called out to us, arms full of calf, asking us to keep him company, saying that his was good toil but lonely, as he was not permitted to ever stand and stroll about.

hans vollman

I explained to him that we were on an urgent mission and must not delay.

roger bevins iii

Mr. Williams (a good sort, never unhappy, always cheerful since his conversion to gentleness) acknowledged that he understood, by waving one hoof of the calf.

hans vollman

XXXVIII.

Soon we approached the massive Collier sick-home, of Italian marble, encircled by three concentric rose gardens, marked, on either side, by an ornate fountain (waterless, now, for winter).

roger bevins iii

When one owns four homes and has fifteen full-time gardeners perfecting one's seven gardens and eight man-made streams, one will, of necessity, spend a great deal of time racing between homes and from garden to garden, and so it is perhaps not surprising if, one afternoon, rushing to check on the progress of a dinner one's cook is preparing for the board of one's favorite charity, one finds oneself compelled to take a little rest, briefly dropping to one knee, then both knees, then pitching forward on to one's face and, unable to rise, proceeding *here* for a more prolonged rest, only to find it not restful at all, since, while ostensibly resting, one finds oneself continually fretting about one's carriages, gardens, furniture, homes, et al., all of which (one hopes) patiently await one's return, not having (Heaven forfend) fallen into the hands of some (reckless, careless, undeserving) Other.

percival "dash" collier

Mr. Collier (shirt clay-stained at the chest from his fall, nose crushed nearly flat) was constantly compelled to float horizontally, like a human compass needle, the top of his head facing in the direction of whichever of his properties he found himself most worried about at the moment.

The top of his head was now facing west. Our arrival causing his worrying to wane, he let out an involuntary gasp of pleasure, bobbed up to vertical, turned to face us.

hans vollman

Mr. Collier, said Mr. Vollman.

Mr. Vollman, said Mr. Collier.

roger bevins iii

A new property-worry then crossing his mind, he was thrown violently forward, stomach down, and, with a grunt of dread, spun to face north.

hans vollman

XXXIX.

Next we must short-cut through that swampy little section populated by our very lowest.

hans vollman

They sought the damp and moonless feeling here.

roger bevins iii

Here stood Mr. Randall and Mr. Twood, in perpetual conversation.

hans vollman

Rendered mutually inarticulate by we knew not what misfortune.

roger bevins iii

Faces reduced to gauzy unreadable smudges.

hans vollman

Torsos gray and shapeless but for the slightest torpedo-shaped suggestion of arms and legs.

roger bevins iii

Indistinguishable except that Mr. Twood's movements retained a touch more vitality. Every now and then, as if making an attempt at persuasion, one of his arm-like appendages would pop up, as if to indicate, on a shelf, something to which he wished to call Mr. Randall's attention.

hans vollman

Mr. Twood having been, we believed, in the retail line.

roger bevins iii

Drag out the big signage Immediately put it away again Drag it out again Not let slip from grasp Significantly reduced women's.

mr. benjamin twood

In response, the gray faceless wedge that had been Mr. Randall would sometimes enact a little dance.

roger bevins iii

Yield the seat Here's a fellow who can really Tinkle the twinklers And the blokeat the piano would proffer his Then it was all me.

jasper randall

Sometimes, near sunrise, when all of the other swamp denizens were weary and depleted and had self-stacked and gone mute near the lightning-blasted black oak, Mr. Randall could be found bowing over and over again, as if to an imagined audience.

roger bevins iii

Leading us to surmise that he must have been a performer of some type.

hans vollman

Thank you thank you thank you!

jasper randall

EXTRAORDINARY VALUE WITHIN:

Only recall your thin weary mother who mightyet be saved By the auto-iron, the cranking grater, the cold-box, the auto-salter, her once-fine posture revived, her winsome kindsmile revived, as of yore, when, in shortknees, you sported a branchsaber among the general pie-odor.

mr. benjamin twood

Slam, arpeggio, pause for smoke drink When I slammed a good one, small ripples would appear in the golden drink set before.

jasper randall

Any admiration we might once have felt for their endurance had long since devolved into revulsion.

roger bevins iii

Were we destined for a similar fate?

hans vollman

We thought not.

roger bevins iii

(Regularly scanned each other's features for any indication of facial-smudging.)

hans vollman

(Continually monitored ourselves for the slightest degradation in diction.)

roger bevins iii

And they were far from the worst.

hans vollman

Consider Mr. Papers.

roger bevins iii

Essentially a cringing gray supine line.

hans vollman

Of whom one would only become aware once one had stumbled over him.

roger bevins iii

Cannery anyhelpmate? Come. To. Heap me? Cannery help? Can any wonder? Help. Conneg ayone heap? Unclog? May?

Place hepMay.

l. b. papers

We had no idea what Mr. Papers might previously have been.

roger bevins iii

There being so little of him remaining.

hans vollman

Go on Move along Else receive an unglad message in your bentover I'll come right up under and ventilate your undertenting.

flanders quinn

Flanders Quinn.

hans vollman

Former robber.

roger bevins iii

Bevins, I'll piss a line of toxic in yr wretched twin wristcuts Gropping you by yr clubdick, Vollman, I'll slang you into the blackfence.

flanders quinn

I, for one, was afraid of him.

roger bevins iii

I was not afraid of him.

Exactly.

But we had urgent business. Must not linger.

hans vollman

And trot-skimmed off along the swamp-margin, Quinn cursing us, then reversing himself and supplicating us to return, as he was frightened to stay in that place, and yet more frightened to leave it (and go), since what must become of a sinner who had slit the throats of a merchant and his daughter beside a broken-wheeled Fredericksburg cariole (plucked the pearls from her very neck and wiped them blood-free with her own silk wrap)?

roger bevins iii

Regaining higher ground we put on the speed, passed through the leaning toolshed, crossed the gravel road, and made good time along the old carriage path, which still retained, to my nostrils, some faint mysterious scent of newsprint.

hans vollman

XL.

Just ahead now, past the slightly left-leaning Cafferty obelisk, a crowd had gathered around a freshly filled sick-hole.

hans vollman

Mr. Vollman approached the group.

Is the new arrival still . . . with us? he delicately inquired.

He is, yes, replied Tobin "Badger" Muller, bent, as always, nearly double with toil.

Shut your traps, so I can hear 'im, barked Mrs. Sparks, on all fours, ear to the ground.

roger bevins iii

XLI.

Wife of my heart laura laura

I take up my pen in a state of such great exhaustion that only my deep love for all of you could so compel me after a day of such Unholy slaughter and fear. And must tel you frankly that Tom Gilman did not make it through the terrible fite. Our position being located in a copse. Much firing during which I heard a cry. Tom is hit & fallen. Our Brave & Noble frend laying upon his Face upon the Ground. I directed the Boys that we would avenge even if it meant stepping through the very gates of Hell.

Such is the state of my Mind that tho I know we set off in that direction & with that Intent, what happened next I cannot recall. Only that all is Well and I embrace my faithful pen to inform you I am at present safe and hope these lines find my Dear little family enjoying the same great Blessing.

I arrived here at this place by Distant journey. And confin'd all the while. It was a terrible fite as I believe I rote you. Tom Gilman is ded as I believe I rote you. But He who preserves or destroys by his Whim saw fit to preserve me to rite these lines to you. To say that although confin'd, I count my Blessings. I am Weary to the point I can scarcely tell where I am or how I got here.

I await the nurse.

Trees hang down. Breece blows. I am somewhat blue & afrade.

O my dear I have a foreboding. And feel I must not linger. In this place of great sadness. He who preserves and Loves us scarcely present. And since we must endeavor always to walk beside Him, I feel I must not linger. But am Confin'd, in Mind & Body, and unable, as if manacled, to leave at this time, dear Wife.

I must seek & seek: What is it that keeps me in this abismal Sad place?

captain william prince

A figure now burst up from the mounded earth, like some wild creature sprung from a cage, and began pacing about, anxiously gazing into the faces of Mr. Muller, Mrs. Sparks, and the others.

roger bevins iii

A soldier.

In uniform.

hans vollman

Don't be afraid, someone drawled from the crowd. You was in that old place, and now you is in this new place here.

roger bevins iii

The soldier became translucent to the point of invisibility, as sometimes happens with us during intense cogitation, and, head first, re-entered the sick-hole.

Then of the instant was out again, look of bleak wonderment upon his face.

hans vollman

Dear wife of my Heart O Laura-Bunny,

Inside my Confin'men is my trapings. I have just now looked. My cheek mole & hareline exact. It is uncomfortable to behold. With a sad look on the (burned!) face. And the torso marred by a grave wound difficult to

I am here, am trapped here and I see of this instant what I must do to get free.

Which is tell the TRUTH & all shall be

O I cant tel shal I tell shall I tell all?

I feel I must or

stay forever

In this drear & awful

Laura send the little ones away & see that they cannot hear what comes next.

I consorted with the smaller of the two. I did. In that rude Hamlet. Consorted with the smaller of the two and she asked after the Loket you had given me and asked Is she a good wife? even as she, atop me, gave a little thrust of the hips and looked me in the eye as to disgrace yr Honor but I assure you that (even as she thrust twise more, eyes still loked on mine) I did not give her that satisfaction, did not sully Yr name or memory, although to serve TRUTH (& thereby escape this place) I feel I must freely confess that as she bent low to proffer her womanly Charms, one of them and then the other to my mouth, asking did my wife do this was my wife as wild? I made an expulsion of breath that we both understood to mean NO my wife does not, my wife is not as Free. And all the further time we consorted there in that dirty leaning shed where her 3 babes did sleep on in there crude crib & her 2 pale Sisters and her Mother did kakle from the Yard, she kept the loket clenched in one hand and, when done, asked could she keep it? But my foul lust now rung out of me, I answered sharply that she could not. And took me to the woods. Where I wept. And there thought with true Tenderness of you. And desided it was kinder to deceive.

To deceive you.

captain william prince

He was pacing a wide stumbling circle now, head in hands.

roger bevins iii

The Moon was high and I said to myself sometimes a man must preserve the peace & spare the One he loves. Which I have done. Until now. I planned to tell you this not in a leter but in person. When perhaps the warmth of the telling might soften the blow. But my situation appearing hopeless in the extreme, my homecoming now never to occur, I tell all to you, cry out to you, in truest voice (I fuked the smaller of the 2, I did, I did it), in hopes that you, and He who hears & forgives all, will hear & forgive all and allow me now to leave this wretched—

captain william prince

Then a blinding flash of light came from near the obelisk, and the familiar, yet always bone-chilling, firesound associated with the matter-lightblooming phenomenon.

roger bevins iii

And he was gone.

hans vollman

His shabby uniform pants raining down, and his shirt, and his boots, and his cheap iron wedding ring.

roger bevins iii

Some of the lesser members of the gathered crowd now began running amok, mocking at the soldier, inflicting various perverse and disrespectful postures upon his sick-mound—not out of meanness, for there is no meanness in them; but rather from excess of feeling.

In this they can be like wild dogs let into a slaughterhouse—racing about upon the spilled blood, driven mad by the certainty that some sort of satisfaction must be near at hand.

hans vollman

My goodness, I thought, poor fellow! You did not give this place a proper chance, but fled it recklessly, leaving behind forever the beautiful things of this world.

And for what?

You do not know.

A most unintelligent wager.

Forgoing eternally, sir, such things as, for example: two fresh-shorn lambs bleat in a new-mown field; four parallel blind-cast linear shadows creep across a sleeping tabby's midday flank; down a bleached-slate roof and into a patch of wilting heather bounce nine gust-loosened acorns; up past a shaving fellow wafts the smell of a warming griddle (and early morning pot-clangs and kitchen-girl chatter); in a nearby harbor a mansion-sized schooner tilts to port, sent so by a flag-rippling, chime-inciting breeze that causes, in a port-side schoolyard, a chorus of childish squeals and the mad barking of what sounds like a dozen—

roger bevins iii

Friend.

Now is hardly the time.

hans vollman

Many apologies.

But (as I believe you must know) the thing is not entirely under my control.

roger bevins iii

The crowd, having suspended its perversities, stood gaping at Mr. Bevins, who had acquired, in the telling, such a bounty of extra eyes, ears, noses, hands, etc., that he now resembled some overstuffed fleshly bouquet.

Bevins applied his usual remedy (closing the eyes and stopping as many of the noses and ears as he could with the various extra hands, dulling, thereby, all sensory intake, thus quieting the mind) and multiple sets of the eyes, ears, noses, and hands retracted or vanished (I could never tell which).

The crowd returned to its abuse of the soldier's sick-mound, "Badger" Muller pretending to piss upon it, Mrs. Sparks squatting over it, screwing her face into an ugly grimace.

Look here, she grunted. I leave the coward a gift.

hans vollman

XLII.

And we proceeded on.

roger bevins iii

Walk-skimming between (or over, when unavoidable) the former home-places of so many fools no longer among us.

hans vollman

Goodson, Raynald, Slocum, Mackey, VanDycke, Piescer, Sliter, Peck, Safko, Swift, Roseboom.

roger bevins iii

For example.

hans vollman

Simkins, Warner, Persons, Lanier, Dunbar, Schuman, Hollingshead, Nelson, Black, VanDuesen.

roger bevins iii

These were, it must be conceded, in the majority, outnumbering our ilk by perhaps an order of magnitude.

hans vollman

Topenbdale, Haggerdown, Messerschmidt, Brown.

roger bevins iii

Underscoring the exceptional qualities of those of us who soldiered on.

hans vollman

Coe, Mumford, Risely, Rowe.

Their places were so quiet, and from these, at dusk, as we whirled out of our respective home-places, nothing whirled out whatsoever, and the contents of their—

roger bevins iii

Sick-boxes.

hans vollman

Lay down there inert, discarded, neglected.

roger bevins iii

Regrettable.

hans vollman

Like discarded horses waiting in vain for beloved riders to return.

roger bevins iii

Edgmont, Tody, Blasingame, Free.

hans vollman

Haberknott, Bewler, Darby, Kerr.

roger bevins iii

These were a chirpy, tepid, desireless sort, generally, and had lingered, if at all, for only the briefest of moments, so completely satisfactory had they found their tenure in that previous place.

hans vollman

Smiling, grateful, gazing about themselves in wonder, favoring us with a last fond look as they—

roger bevins iii

Surrendered.

hans vollman

Succumbed.

roger bevins iii

Capitulated.

hans vollman

XLIII.

We found the gentleman as had been described to us, near Bellingwether, *Husband, Father, Shipwright.*

hans vollman

Sitting cross-legged and defeated in a patch of tall grass.

roger bevins iii

As we approached, he lifted head from hands and heaved a great sigh. He might have been, in that moment, a sculpture on the theme of Loss.

hans vollman

Shall we? Mr. Vollman said.
I hesitated.
The Reverend would not approve, I said.
The Reverend is not here, he said.

roger bevins iii

XLIV.

In order to occupy the greatest percentage of the gentleman's volume, I lowered myself into his lap and sat cross-legged, just as he was sitting.

hans vollman

The two now comprised one sitting man, Mr. Vollman's greater girth somewhat overflowing the gentleman, his massive member existing wholly outside the gentleman, pointing up at the moon.

roger bevins iii

It was quite something.
Quite something in there.
Bevins, come in! I called out. This is not to be missed.

hans vollman

I went in, assuming the same cross-legged posture.

roger bevins iii

And the three of us were one.

hans vollman

So to speak.

roger bevins iii

XLV.

There was a touch of prairie about the fellow.

hans vollman

Yes.

roger bevins iii

Like stepping into a summer barn late at night.

hans vollman

Or a musty plains office, where some bright candle still burns.

roger bevins iii

Vast. Windswept. New. Sad.

hans vollman

Spacious. Curious. Doom-minded. Ambitious.

roger bevins iii

Back slightly out.

hans vollman

Right boot chafing.

roger bevins iii

The recent entry of the (youthful) Mr. Bevins now caused the gentleman a mild thought-swerve back to a scene from his own (wild) youth:

a soft-spoken but retrograde (dirty cheeks, kind eyes) lass leading him shyly down a muddy path, nettles accruing on her swaying green skirt as, in his mind, at the time, a touch of shame rose up, having to do with his sense that this girl was not really fair game, i.e., was more beast than lady, i.e., did not even know how to read.

hans vollman

Becoming aware of that which he was remembering, the man's face reddened (we could feel it reddening) at the thought that he was (in the midst of this tragic circumstance) remembering such a sordid incident.

roger bevins iii

And he hurriedly directed his (*our*) mind elsewhere, so as to leave this inappropriate thought behind.

hans vollman

XLVI.

Tried to "see" his boy's face.

roger bevins iii

Couldn't.

hans vollman

Tried to "hear" the boy's laugh.

roger bevins iii

Couldn't.

hans vollman

Attempted to recall some particular incident involving the boy, in hope this might—

roger bevins iii

First time we fitted him for a suit.

Thus thought the gentleman.

(This did the trick.)

First time we fitted him for a suit, he looked down at the trousers and then up at me, amazed, as if to say: Father, I am wearing grown-up pants.

Shirtless, barefoot, pale round belly like an old man's. Then the little cuffed shirt and buttoning it up.

Goodbye, little belly, we are enshirting you now.

Enshirting? I do not believe that is even a word, Father.

I tied the little tie. Spun him around for a look.

We have dressed up a wild savage, looks like, I said.

He made the growling face. His hair stuck straight up, his cheeks were red. (Racing around that store just previous, he had knocked over a rack of socks.) The tailor, complicit, brought out the little jacket with much pomp.

Then the shy boyish smile as I slid the jacket on him.

Say, he said, don't I look fine, Father?

Then no thought at all for a while, and we just looked about us: bare trees black against the dark-blue sky.

Little jacket little jacket little jacket.

This phrase sounded in our head.

A star flickered off, then on.

Same one he is wearing back in there, now.

Huh.

Same little jacket. But he who is wearing it is—

(I so want it not to be true.)

Broken.

Pale broken thing.

Why will it not work. What magic word made it work. Who is the keeper of that word. What did it profit Him to switch this one off. What a contraption it is. How did it ever run. What spark ran it. Grand little machine. Set up just so. Receiving the spark, it jumped to life.

What put out that spark? What a sin it would be. Who would dare. Ruin such a marvel. Hence is murder anathema. God forbid I should ever commit such a grievous—

hans vollman

Something then troubling us—

roger bevins iii

We ran one hand roughly over our face, as if attempting to suppress a notion just arising.

hans vollman

This effort not proving successful—

roger bevins iii

The notion washed over us.

hans vollman

XLVII.

Young Willie Lincoln was laid to rest on the day that the casualty lists from the Union victory at Fort Donelson were publicly posted, an event that caused a great shock among the public at that time, the cost in life being unprecedented thus far in the war.

In "Setting the Record Straight: Memoir, Error, and Evasion," by Jason Tumm, "Journal of American History."

The details of the losses were communicated to the President even as young Willie lay under embalmment.

Iverness, op. cit.

More than a thousand troops on both sides were killed and three times that number wounded. It was "a most bloody fight," a young Union soldier told his father, so devastating to his company that despite the victory, he remained "sad, lonely and down-hearted." Only seven of the eighty-five men in his unit survived.

Goodwin, op. cit.

The dead at Donelson, sweet Jesus. Heaped and piled like threshed wheat, one on top of two on top of three. I walked through it after with a bad feeling. Lord it was me done that, I thought.

In "These Battle Memories," by First Lieutenant Daniel Brower.

A thousand dead. That was something new. It seemed a real war now.

In "The Great War, as Described by Its Warriors," by Marshall Turnbull.

The dead lay as they had fallen, in every conceivable shape, some grasping their guns as though they were in the act of firing, while others, with a cartridge in their icy grasp, were in the act of loading. Some of the countenances wore a peaceful, glad smile, while on others rested a fiendish look of hate. It looked as though each countenance was the exact counterpart of the thoughts that were passing through the mind when the death messenger laid them low. Perhaps that noble-looking youth, with his smiling up-turned face, with his glossy ringlets matted with his own life-blood, felt a mother's prayer stealing over his senses as his young life went out. Near him lay a young husband with a prayer for his wife and little one yet lingering on his lips. Youth and age, virtue and evil, were represented on those ghastly countenances. Before us lay the charred and blackened remains of some who had been burnt alive. They were wounded too badly to move and the fierce elements consumed them.

In "The Civil War Years: A Day-by-Day Chronicle of the Life of a Nation," edited by Robert E. Denney, account of Corporal Lucius W. Barber, Co. D, 15th Illinois Volunteer Infantry, combatant at Fort Donelson.

I had never seen a dead person before. Now I saw my fill. One poor lad had frozen solid in the posture of looking down aghast at his wound, eyes open. Some of his insides had spilled out and made, there on his side, under a thin coat of ice, a blur of purple and red. At home on my dressing table was a holy card of the Sacred Heart of Jesus, and this fellow looked like that, only his bulge of red and purple was lower and larger and off to one side and him gazing down at it in horror.

In "That Terrible Glory: A Collection of Civil War Letters from the Men Who Fought It," compiled and edited by Brian Bell and Libby Trust.

And Mother fire had swep through the frozen dead and hurt where they lay. We found one still kicking among them and was able to bring him back still alive not even knowing which side he was on, so burned was he, and naked except for one leg of his pants. I never did hear how he made out. But it did not look hopeful for that poor divil.

In "Letters of an Illinois Soldier," edited by Sam Westfall, account of Private Edward Gates, Co. F, 15th Illinois Volunteer Infantry.

Two or three of us would grab a fellow and haul him away just as we found him, as it was cold and the bodies were completely froze. That day I learned a person can get used to anything. Soon it all seemed normal to us, and we even joked about it, making up names for each, depending on how it looked. There was Bent-Over, there was Shocked, this was Half-Boy.

Brower, op. cit.

We found two little fellers holding hands couldn't been more than fourteen fifteen apiece as if they had desided to pass through that dark portel together.

Gates, op. cit.

How miny more ded do you attend to make sir afore you is done? One minit there was our litle Nate on that bridge with a fishpole and ware is that boy now? And who is it called him hither, in that Notice he saw down to Orbys, wellsir, that was your name he saw upon it "Abaham Lincoln."

In "Country Letters to President Lincoln," compiled and edited by Josephine Banner and Evelyn Dressman, letter from Robert Hansworthy, Boonsboro, Maryland.

XLVIII.

He is just one.

And the weight of it about to kill me.

Have exported this grief. Some three thousand times. So far. To date. A mountain. Of boys. Someone's boys. Must keep on with it. May not have the heart for it. One thing to pull the lever when blind to the result. But here lies one dear example of what I accomplish by the orders I—

May not have the heart for it.

What to do. Call a halt? Toss down the loss-hole those three thousand? Sue for peace? Become great course-reversing fool, king of indecision, laughing-stock for the ages, waffling hick, slim Mr. Turnabout?

It is out of control. Who is doing it. Who caused it. Whose arrival on the scene began it.

What am I doing.

What am I doing here.

Everything nonsense now. Those mourners came up. Hands extended. Sons intact. Wearing on their faces enforced sadness-masks to hide any sign of their happiness, which—which went on. They could not hide how alive they yet were with it, with their happiness at the potential of their still-living sons. Until lately I was one of them. Strolling whistling through the slaughterhouse, averting my eyes from the carnage, able to laugh and dream and hope because it had not yet happened to me.

To us.

Trap. Horrible trap. At one's birth it is sprung. Some last day must arrive. When you will need to get out of this body. Bad enough. Then we bring a baby here. The terms of the trap are compounded. That baby also must de-

part. All pleasures should be tainted by that knowledge. But hopeful dear us, we forget.

Lord, what is this? All of this walking about, trying, smiling, bowing, joking? This sitting-down-at-table, pressing-of-shirts, tying-of-ties, shining-of-shoes, planning-of-trips, singing-of-songs-in-the-bath?

When he is to be left out here?

Is a person to nod, dance, reason, walk, discuss?

As before?

A parade passes. He can't rise and join. Am I to run after it, take my place, lift knees high, wave a flag, blow a horn?

Was he dear or not?

Then let me be happy no more.

hans vollman

XLIX.

It was quite cold. (Being in the gentleman, we were, for the first time in—

hans vollman

Ever so long.

roger bevins iii

Quite cold ourselves.)

hans vollman

He sat, distraught and shivering, seeking about for any consolation.

He must either be in a happy place, or some null place by now.

Thought the gentleman.

In either case is no longer suffering.

Suffered so terribly at the end.

(The racking cough the trembling the vomiting the pathetic attempts to keep the mouth wiped with a shaky hand the way his panicked eyes would steal up and catch mine as if to say is there really nothing Papa you can do?)

And in his mind the gentleman stood (we stood with him) on a lonely plain, screaming at the top of *our* lungs.

Quiet then, and a great weariness.

All over now. He is either in joy or nothingness.

(So why grieve?

The worst of it, for him, is over.)

Because I loved him so and am in the habit of loving him and that love must take the form of fussing and worry and doing.

Only there is nothing left to do.

Free myself of this darkness as I can, remain useful, not go mad.

Think of him, when I do, as being in some bright place, free of suffering, resplendent in a new mode of being.

Thus thought the gentleman.

Thoughtfully combing a patch of grass with his hand.

roger bevins iii

L.

Sad.

roger bevins iii

Very sad.

hans vollman

Especially given what we knew.

roger bevins iii

His boy was not "in some bright place, free of suffering."

hans vollman

No.

roger bevins iii

Not "resplendent in a new mode of being."

hans vollman

Au contraire.

roger bevins iii

Above us, an errant breeze loosened many storm-broken branches.

hans vollman

Which fell to the earth at various distances.

roger bevins iii

As if the woods were full of newly roused creatures.

hans vollman

I wonder, said Mr. Vollman.

And I knew what was coming.

roger bevins iii

LI.

We wished the lad to go, and thereby save himself. His father wished him to be "in some bright place, free of suffering, resplendent in a new mode of being."

A happy confluence of wishes.

It seemed we must persuade the gentleman to return with us to the white stone home. Once there, we must encourage the lad into the gentleman, hoping that, while therein, having overheard his father's wish, he would be convinced to—

hans vollman

A fine idea, I said. But we have no method by which to accomplish it.

roger bevins iii

(There has historically been some confusion around this issue.)

hans vollman

No confusion at all, friend.

It is simply not within our power to communicate with those of that ilk, much less persuade them to *do* anything.

And I think you know it.

roger bevins iii

LII.

I beg to differ.

We caused a wedding once, if you will recall.

hans vollman

Highly debatable.

roger bevins iii

A couple strolling here, on the brink of ending their engagement, reversed their decision, under our influence.

hans vollman

Almost certainly a coincidence.

roger bevins iii

Several of us—Hightower, the three of us, and—what was his name? The decapitated fellow?

hans vollman

Ellers.

roger bevins iii

Ellers, of course!

Bored, we swarmed and entered that couple and, through the combined force of our concentrated wishfulness, were able to effect—

hans vollman

This much is true:

They were overcome with sudden passion and retreated behind one of the stone homes.

roger bevins iii

To act upon said passion.

hans vollman

While we watched.

roger bevins iii

I have misgivings about that. The watching.

hans vollman

Well, you had no misgivings on that day, my dear fellow. Your member was swollen to an astonishing size. And even on a normal day, it is swollen to—

roger bevins iii

I seem to remember you watching as well. I do not recall the slightest aversion of any of your many, many—

hans vollman

Truly, it was invigorating to see such passion.

The fury of their embraces was remarkable.

roger bevins iii

Yes.

They sent birds winging from the trees with their terrific moans of pleasure.

hans vollman

After which they renewed their commitment and departed hand in hand, reconciled, betrothed again.

roger bevins iii

And we had done it.

hans vollman

Come now. They were young, lustful, alone in an isolated spot, on a beautiful spring night. They hardly needed any help from—

roger bevins iii

Friend:

We are here.

Already here.

Within.

A train approaches a wall at a fatal rate of speed. You hold a switch in your hand, that accomplishes you know not what: do you throw it? Disaster is otherwise assured.

It costs you nothing.

Why not try?

hans vollman

LIII.

There in the gentleman, Mr. Bevins reached for my hand.

hans vollman

And we began.

roger bevins iii

To persuade the gentleman.

hans vollman

To attempt to persuade him.

roger bevins iii

Together, the two of us began to think of the white stone home.

hans vollman

Of the boy.

roger bevins iii

His face, his hair, his voice.

hans vollman

His gray suit.

roger bevins iii

Turned-in feet.

hans vollman

Scuffed shoes.

roger bevins iii

Stand up, go back, we thought as one. *Your boy requires your counsel.*

hans vollman

He is in grave danger.

roger bevins iii

It is anathema for children to tarry here.

hans vollman

His headstrong nature, a virtue in that previous place, imperils him here, where the natural law, harsh and arbitrary, brooks no rebellion, and must be scrupulously obeyed.

roger bevins iii

We request, therefore, that you rise.

hans vollman

And return with us, to save your boy.

roger bevins iii

It did not seem to be working.

hans vollman

The gentleman just *sat,* combing the grass, rather blank-minded.

roger bevins iii

It seemed we must be more direct.

hans vollman

We turned our minds, by mutual assent, to a certain shared memory of Miss Traynor.

roger bevins iii

Christmas last, paying a holiday visit, we found that, under the peculiar strain of that blessed holiday, she had gone *beyond* the fallen bridge, the vulture, the large dog, the terrible hag gorging on black cake, the stand of flood-ravaged corn, the umbrella ripped open by a wind we could not feel—

hans vollman

And was manifesting as an ancient convent, containing fifteen bitter quarreling nuns, about to burn to the ground.

roger bevins iii

A girl-sized convent in the style of Agreda, the little nuns inside her just embarking on morning vespers.

hans vollman

Suddenly, the place (the girl) is ablaze: screams, shrieks, grunts, vows renounced if only one might be saved.

roger bevins iii

But none are saved, all are lost.

hans vollman

We willed ourselves to see it again, smell it again, hear it again: the incense; the fragrant wall-lining sage-bushes; the rose-scented breeze wafting down from the hill; the shrill nun-screams; the padding of the tiny nun-feet against the packed red clay of the town-bound trail—

roger bevins iii

Nothing.

hans vollman

He just sat.

roger bevins iii

Now, together, we became aware of something.

hans vollman

In his left trouser pocket.

roger bevins iii

A lock.

hans vollman

The lock. From the white stone home.

roger bevins iii

Heavy and cold.
Key still in it.

hans vollman

He had forgotten to rehang it.

roger bevins iii

An opportunity to simplify our argument.

hans vollman

We focused our attention upon the lock.

roger bevins iii

Upon the perils of *an unlocked door.*

hans vollman

I called to mind Fred Downs, raging in frustration as those drunken Anatomy students tossed his bagged sick-form on to their cart, horses rearing with alarm at the smell.

roger bevins iii

I pictured the wolf-rended torso of Mrs. Scoville, tilted against her doorframe, one arm torn away, little veil fluttering in what remained of her white hair.

Imagined the wolves massing in the woods even now, sniffing the breeze—

Making for the white stone home.

Snarling, drooling.

Bursting in.

Etc.

hans vollman

The gentleman put his hand into that pocket.

roger bevins iii

Closed it upon the lock.

hans vollman

Shook his head unhappily:

How could I have forgotten such a simple—

roger bevins iii

Got to his feet.

hans vollman

And walked off.

roger bevins iii

In the direction of the white stone home.

hans vollman

Leaving Mr. Vollman and me there behind him on the ground.

roger bevins iii

LIV.

Had we—had we done it?

hans vollman

It seemed that perhaps we had.

roger bevins iii

LV.

Because we were as yet intermingled with one another, traces of Mr. Vollman naturally began arising in my mind and traces of me naturally began arising in his.

roger bevins iii

Never having found ourselves in that configuration before—

hans vollman

This effect was an astonishment.

roger bevins iii

I saw, as if for the first time, the great beauty of the things of this world: waterdrops in the woods around us plopped from leaf to ground; the stars were low, blue-white, tentative; the wind-scent bore traces of fire, dryweed, rivermuck; the tssking drybush rattles swelled with a peaking breeze, as some distant cross-creek sleigh-nag tossed its neck-bells.

hans vollman

I saw his Anna's face, and understood his reluctance to leave her behind.

roger bevins iii

I desired the man-smell and the strong hold of a man.

hans vollman

I knew the printing press, loved operating it. (Knew *platen*, *roller-hook*, *gripper-bar*, *chase-bed*.) Recalled my disbelief, as the familiar center-beam came down. That fading final panicked instant! I have crashed through my desk with my chin; someone (Mr. Pitts) screams from the ante-room, my bust of Washington lies about me, shattered.

roger bevins iii

The stove ticks. In my thrashing panic I have upended a chair. The blood, channeled within the floorboard interstices, pools against the margins of the next-room rug. I may yet be revived. Who has not made a mistake? The world is kind, it forgives, it is full of second chances. When I broke Mother's vase, I was allowed to sweep the fruit cellar. When I spoke unkindly to Sophia, our maid, I wrote her a letter, and all was well.

hans vollman

As soon as tomorrow, if I can only recover, I will have her. I will sell the shop. We will travel. In many new cities, I will see her in dresses of many colors. Which will drop to many floors. Friends already, we will become much more: will work, every day, to "expand the frontiers of our happiness" (as she once so beautifully put it). And—there may be children yet: I am not so old, only forty-six, and she is in the prime of her—

roger bevins iii

Why had we not done this before?

hans vollman

So many years I had known this fellow and yet had never really known him at all.

roger bevins iii

It was intensely pleasurable.

hans vollman

But was not helping.

roger bevins iii

The gentleman was gone.

Headed back to the white stone home.

hans vollman

Impelled by us!

roger bevins iii

O wonderful night!

hans vollman

I exited Mr. Vollman.

roger bevins iii

Upon Mr. Bevins's exit, I was immediately filled with longing for him and his associated phenomena, a longing that rivaled the longing I had felt for my parents when I first left their home for my apprenticeship in Baltimore—a considerable longing indeed.

Such had been the intensity of our co-habitation.

I would never fail to fully see him again: dear Mr. Bevins!

hans vollman

Dear Mr. Vollman!

I looked at him; he looked at me.

roger bevins iii

We would be infused with some trace of one another forevermore.

hans vollman

But that was not all.

roger bevins iii

We seemed, now, to know the gentleman as well.

hans vollman

Removed from both Vollman and the gentleman, I felt arising within me a body of startling new knowledge. The gentleman? Was *Mr. Lincoln*. Mr. Lincoln was *President*. How could it be? How could it not be? And yet I knew with all my heart that Mr. Taylor was President.

roger bevins iii

That Mr. Polk occupied that esteemed office.

hans vollman

And yet I knew with all my heart that Mr. Lincoln was President. We were at war. We were not at war. All was chaos. All was calm. A device had been invented for distant communication. No such device existed. Nor ever could. The notion was mad. And yet I had seen it, had used it; could hear, in my mind, the sound it made as it functioned.

It was: *telegraph*.

My God!

roger bevins iii

On the day of the beam, Polk had been President. But now, I knew (with a dazzling clarity) that Polk had been succeeded by *Taylor*, and Taylor by *Fillmore*, and Fillmore by *Pierce*—

hans vollman

After which, *Pierce* had been succeded by *Buchanan*, and *Buchanan* by—

roger bevins iii

Lincoln!

hans vollman

President Lincoln!

roger bevins iii

The rail line ran beyond Buffalo now—

hans vollman

Far beyond!

roger bevins iii

The Duke of York nightcap is no longer worn. There is something called the "slashed Pamela sleeve."

hans vollman

The theaters are lit now with gaslight. *Striplights* and *groundrows* being employed in this process.

roger bevins iii

The resulting spectacle is a wonder.

hans vollman

Has revolutionized the theater.

roger bevins iii

The facial expressions of the actors are seen most clearly.

hans vollman

Allowing for an entirely new level of realism in the performance.

roger bevins iii

It would be difficult to express the perplexity these revelations thrust upon us.

hans vollman

We turned and ran-skimmed back toward the white stone home, talking most excitedly.

roger bevins iii

Mr. Bevins's hair and numerous eyes, hands, and noses velocity-streaming behind him.

hans vollman

Mr. Vollman bearing his tremendous member in his hands, so as not to trip himself on it.

roger bevins iii

Soon we were in Mr. Lincoln's lee, so close we could smell him.

hans vollman

Soap, pomade, pork, coffee, smoke.

roger bevins iii

Milk, incense, leather.

hans vollman

TWO

LVI.

The night of February 25, 1862, was cold but clear, a welcome respite from the terrible weather the Capital city had been experiencing. Willie Lincoln was now interred, and all ceremonial activities associated with that activity concluded. The nation held its breath, hopeful the President could competently reassume the wheel of the ship of state in this, its hour of greatest need.

In "The Spiritual Lincoln:
An Essential Journey," by C. R. DePage.

LVII.

By two a.m. the President had not yet returned to the White House. I considered waking Mrs. Lincoln. Although it was not unusual for the President to ride out alone evenings. He would routinely refuse any escort. Tonight he had ridden Little Jack, of whom he was fond. The night was cold and wet. He had not taken his greatcoat, which still hung on the peg. He would be chilled when he returned, that much was certain. Although his constitution was strong. I took up my post near the door, now and then stepping out to listen for Little Jack's trod. Another half hour passed and still no Mr. Lincoln. If I were in his shoes, I thought, I might keep riding and never come back, until I had ridden myself back West into a life of less import and trouble. When three a.m. had come and gone I began to think he might have done just that.

I again considered waking Mrs. Lincoln. But pity forbade me. She was in a very poor state. I found it strange that he should have left her alone at such a time. But she was heavily sedated and, I think, not aware that he was gone.

Hilyard, op. cit., account of
Paul Riles, White House guard.

LVIII.

Mary Lincoln's mental health had never been good, and the loss of young Willie ended her life as a functional wife and mother.

In "A Mother's Trial: Mary Lincoln and the Civil War," by Jayne Coster.

Around two in the afternoon I heard a terrible commotion from the part of the house where the sick child lay. It appeared the moment had come. Mrs Lincoln rushed past me, head lowered, making a sound I have never heard emitted from human throat, before or since.

Hilyard, op. cit., account of Sophie Lenox, maid.

While the president's outburst allowed for depiction, his wife's did not.

Epstein, op. cit.

The pale face of her dead boy threw her into convulsions.

Keckley, op. cit.

Mary Lincoln collapsed into her bed.

Von Drehle, op. cit.

An altered woman.

Keckley, op. cit.

Laudanum being administered, even this powerful concoction could not suppress her cries of agony or subdue her disbelieving outrage.

Coster, op. cit.

Mrs. Lincoln was too ill to attend the funeral services.

Leech, op. cit.

Mary Lincoln stayed abed for a full ten days following the funeral.

In "A Belle Remade: The Journey of Mary Lincoln," by Kevin Swarney.

Mrs. Lincoln was unable to leave her room or rise from bed for many weeks after the tragedy.

Sloane, op. cit.

When she finally emerged a month later, she moved about mechanically, gazing at us as if we were strangers.

Hilyard, op. cit., account of D. Strumphort, butler.

Some blows fall too heavy upon those too fragile.

Coster, op. cit.

There she lay, longing that the thing should not be so; now disbelieving that it had occurred, now convinced anew that it had. Always the same walls, bed-things, cup, ceiling, windows. She could not rise and leave—the world outside too terrible now. She sipped of the drugged drink that was her only hope for peace.

Swarney, op. cit.

Where was her boy? she kept asking. Where was he? Couldn't someone find him, bring him to her at once? Mustn't he yet be *somewhere*?

Hilyard, op. cit., account of Sophie Lenox, maid.

LIX.

All still quiet, dear Brother—Only the fire popping & dear Grace snoring from your old room, where I have put her, so she may more easily attend me on these difficult nights—The moonlight shows the premises across the way littered far & wide with the detritus of yesterday's great storm—Mighty tree-limbs lay against crypts & across graves—You may recall a certain statue of a bald man in Roman garb (whom we used to call "Morty"), standing with one foot on the neck of a snake, & that once a certain mischievous young fellow threw his sweater up there many times, until "Morty" might catch it upon the end of his sword—Well, "Morty" is no more—Or at least is not the man he once was—A falling limb hit that brave Roman at the arm, & off it came, sword & all, taking off the head of the snake on its way down—Now arm & sword & snakehead lie in a heap—& Morty himself, as if shaken by this proof of his mortality, stands a bit askew on his base.

Must have dozed a bit just now—Yes it is nearly four—There is a horse over there, across the way, tied to the cemetery fence—A calm & exhausted fellow, nodding as if to say: Well, though I find myself at the yard of the Dead in the dark of night, I am Horse, & must obey.

So now I have a mystery to distract me—Who could be over there at such a late hour?—Some young gentleman, I hope, paying homage to a true love lost.

The light burns in Manders's little guard-house and he paces back & forth before the window, as is his habit—You may recall that it was he who mounted a ladder to retrieve the afore-mentioned sweater from Morty's sword—He is older now & looks it, burdened, I think, with many family concerns—And now leaves the guard-house—His lantern-light receding—He is seeking, I imagine, our "midnight visitor"—All very intriguing—Whoever might think that an impairment such as mine disallows excitement, I wish that individual could sit here beside me at this window tonight—I will stay awake, I think, & see if I may glimpse the face of our visitor once Manders retrieves the fellow.

Perkins, op. cit.

LX.

Left behind on the roof of the white stone home, I resolved to make one final attempt to talk sense to the boy, who lay nearly insensate at my feet, like a dazed and fallen Pasha-prince.

My feelings had been hurt by the juvenile, deceptive actions of Mr. Bevins and Mr. Vollman, who, in their rush to chase after the slightest amusement, had left me in a very bad position indeed. Like some sort of primitive gardener I worked, bent at the waist, seizing at tendrils with both hands. I must continually be deciding whether to attack the several already attached, or take on their new-arising brethren. In truth, it mattered not what I did: the boy's time was not long.

An opportunity soon presented for a frank moment with him.

Scanning the horizon for the feckless Bevins and Vollman, I saw instead, creeping out of the woods, the Crutcher brothers, accompanied, as usual, by Mr. and Mrs. Reedy, the four of them comprising the core group of that depraved orgiastic cohort that resided near the flagpole.

We come to watch, said Matt Crutcher.

The decline, said Richard Crutcher.

It is of interest to us, said Mrs. Reedy.

We watched it last time, said Matt Crutcher. With that gal.

Found it most stimulating, said Mr. Reedy.

Really gave us a boost, said Mrs. Reedy.

And everyone needs a boost, said Mr. Reedy.

In this dung-hole, said Matt Crutcher.

Don't judge us, said Mr. Reedy.

Or do, said Mrs. Reedy.

Makes us feel naughtier, said Matt Crutcher.

To each their own, said Richard Crutcher, stepping over close to Mrs. Reedy.

Perhaps, said Mrs. Reedy, slipping her hand into his pants-pocket.

The group now fell into a watchful rapacious squat: disgusting vultures drawn here by the boy's misfortune. And soon got up to some strange cross-handed business, manifesting as one terrible creature, their pumping arms and rhythmic gasping conveying a distinctly mechanical impression.

What do you think? I said to the boy. Is this a good place? A healthy place? Do these people seem sane to you, and worthy of emulation?

And yet here you are, the boy said.

I am different, I said.

From me? he said.

From everyone, I said.

Different how? he said.

And I teetered on the brink of telling him.

the reverend everly thomas

LXI.

For I *am* different, yes.

Unlike *these* (Bevins, Vollman, the dozens of other naifs I reside here among), I know very well what I am.

Am not "sick," not "lying on a kitchen floor," not "being healed via sick-box," not "waiting to be revived."

No.

Even there, at the end, in our guest room, with a view of the bricks of the Rednell house next door, upon which there hung a flowering vine (it was early June), the stable and grateful state of mind I had tried to cultivate all my life, via my ministry, left me in a state of acceptance and obedience, and I knew very well what I was.

I was dead.

I felt the urge to go.

I went.

Yes: simultaneously becoming cause and (awed) observer (from within) of the bone-chilling firesound associated with the matterlight-blooming phenomenon (an experience I shall not even attempt to describe), I went.

And found myself walking along a high-mountain trail, preceded by two men who, I understood, had passed only seconds before. One wore a funeral suit of a very cheap type, and looked this way and that, like a tourist, and was, rather oddly, humming, in a way that communicated a sense of vacuous happiness, willful ignorance. Though he was dead, his attitude seemed to be: Ha ha, what's all this, then? The other wore a yellow bathing costume, had a beard of flaming red, moved along angrily, as if in a hurry to get somewhere he very much resented going.

The former man was from Pennsylvania; the latter from Maine (Bangor or thereabouts); had spent much time in farmfields and often made his way to the coast, to sit for hours on the rocks.

He wore a bathing costume because he had drowned while swimming.

Somehow I knew this.

Periodically, as I made my way down that trail, I was also back *here*. Was in my grave; was startled *out* of my grave by the sight of what lay in my coffin (that prim-looking, dry-faced relic); was *above* my grave, nervously walk-skimming about it.

My wife and congregation were saying their final goodbyes, their weeping driving small green daggers into me: literal daggers. With each sob, a dagger left the griever and found its way into me, most painfully.

Then I was back *there*, upon that trail, with my two friends. Below us lay a distant valley that I somehow knew to be our destination. A set of stone steps became visible. My companions paused, glanced back. Recognizing me as a man of God (I had been buried in my vestments) they seemed to be asking: Should we proceed?

I indicated that we should.

From the valley below: chanting of some sort, excited voices, the clanging of a bell. These sounds contented me; we had journeyed, had arrived, the festivities might now begin. I was filled with happiness that my life had been judged worthy of such a spectacular denouement.

Then, vexingly, I was back *here;* my wife and congregation now departing in coaches, occasionally sending forth the random green dagger, the impact of which did not lessen no matter how far they drove. Soon my mourners had crossed the Potomac, and were eating the funeral meal at Prevey's. I knew this even as I paced back and forth before my grave. I became panicked at the prospect of becoming stranded *here*, wished only to rejoin my friends *there*, on that stairway. *This* place was now entirely unappealing: a boneyard, a charnel ground, a garbage dump, a sad remnant of a discouraging and grossly material nightmare from which I was only just waking.

Instantaneously (with that very thought) I was *there* again, with my friends, coming off those stairs into a sun-drenched meadow in which stood a large structure unlike any I had ever seen, built of interlocking planks and wedges of purest diamond, giving off an array of colors that changed of the instant with any slight variation in the quality of the sunshine.

We approached arm in arm. A crowd gathered about us, ushering us along. An honor guard stood by the door, beaming at our approach.

The door flew open.

Inside, a vast expanse of diamond floor led to a single diamond table at which sat a man I knew to be a prince; not Christ, but Christ's direct emissary. The room was reminiscent of Hartley's warehouse, a place I had known as a boy: a tremendous open space, high-ceilinged and forbidding, made more forbidding by the presence of an authority figure (Hartley himself, in those early days; that Christ-emissary now) seated near a source of heat and light (a fireplace then; a jagged topaz now, on fire from within, upon a stand of pure gold).

We understood that we were to step forth in our previous order.

Our red-bearded friend, ridiculous in his bathing costume, went first.

Appearing now from either side, walking in perfect step with him as he approached the table, were two beings, beautiful in appearance: tall, thin, luminous, borne on feet of sun-yellow light.

How did you live? one asked.

Tell it truthfully, the other said, as, from either side, they gently touched their heads to his.

Both beamed with pleasure at what they found within.

May we confirm? said the one on the right.

Sure, said our red-bearded friend. And I hope you will, too.

The yellow-footed being on the right sang out a single joyful note and several smaller versions of himself *danced* out (I use this word to denote the utter grace of their movements) bearing a large mirror, the edges of which were encrusted with precious gems.

The yellow-footed being on the left sang *his* single joyful note, and several smaller versions of himself tumbled out, rolling forth in the most exquisite sequence of gymnastic movements imaginable, bearing a scale.

Quick check, said Christ's emissary from his seat at the diamond table.

The being on the right held the mirror up before the red-bearded fellow. The being on the left reached into the red-bearded man's chest and, with a deft and somehow *apologetic* movement, extracted the man's heart, and placed it on the scale.

The being on the right checked the mirror. The being on the left checked the scale.

Very good, said the Christ-emissary.

We are so happy for you, said the being on the right, and I cannot adequately describe the sound of rejoicing that echoed then from across what I now understood to be a vast kingdom extending in all directions around the palace.

A tremendous set of diamond doors at the far end of the hall flew open, revealing an even vaster hall.

I perceived, there within, a tent of purest white silk (although to describe it thus is to defame it—this was no earthly silk, but a higher, more perfect variety, of which our silk is a laughable imitation), within which a great feast was about to unfold, and on a raised dais sat our host, a magnificent king, and next to the king's place sat an empty chair (a grand chair, upholstered with gold, if gold were spun of light and each particle of that light exuded joy and the sound of joy), and that chair was intended, I understood, for our red-bearded friend.

Christ was that king within; Christ was also (I now saw) that seated prince/emissary at the table, in disguise, or secondary emanation.

I cannot explain it.

The red-bearded man passed through the diamond doors in his characteristic rolling gait and the doors closed behind him.

Never in my nearly eighty years of life on earth had I experienced a greater or more bitter contrast between *happiness* (the happiness I felt even glimpsing that exalted tent, from such a great distance) and *sadness* (I was not within the tent, and even a few seconds without seemed a dreadful eternity).

I began to weep, as did my funeral-suited friend from Pennsylvania.

But his weeping at least was leavened with anticipation: for he was next, his separation from that place to be that much briefer than mine.

He stepped forward.

How did you live? asked the being on the right.

Tell it truthfully, the other said, as, from either side, they gently touched their heads to his.

They recoiled, then withdrew to two gray stone pots set down on either side of that grand hall, into which they vomited twin streams of brightly colored fluid.

The small versions of themselves rushed to bring towels, upon which they wiped their mouths.

May we confirm? said the one on the right.

Wait, what did you see, he said. Is there some—

But it was too late.

The being on the right sang a single ominous note and out came the several smaller versions of himself, but crippled and grimacing, bearing between them a feces-encrusted mirror. The being on the left sang his (somber, jarring) note, and several smaller versions of himself tumbled out, rolling forth via a series of spastic clumsy gymnastic movements that were somehow *accusatory*, bearing the scale.

Quick check, the Christ-prince said sternly.

I'm not sure I completely understood the instructions, the funeral-suited man said. If I might be allowed to—

The being on the right held the mirror up before the funeral-suited man, and the being on the left reached into the funeral-suited man's chest with a deft and *aggressive* movement, extracted the man's heart, and placed it on the scale.

Oh dear, said the Christ-emissary.

A sound of horrific opprobrium and mourning echoed all across that kingdom.

The diamond doors flew open.

I blinked in disbelief at the transformation within. The tent was no longer of silk but flesh (speckled and pink with spoiled blood); the feast was not a feast, but, rather, on long tables inside, numerous human forms were stretched out, in various stages of flaying; the host was no king, no Christ, but a beast, bloody-handed and long-fanged, wearing a sulfur-colored robe, bits of innards speckling it. Visible therein were three women and a bent-backed old man, bearing long ropes of (their own) intestines (terrible!), but most terrible of all was the way they screeched with joy as my funeral-suited friend was dragged in among them, and the way that poor fellow kept smiling, as if attempting to ingratiate himself with his captors, listing the many charitable things he had done back in Pennsylvania, and the numerous good people who would vouch for him, especially in the vicinity of Wilkes-Barre, if only they might be summoned, even as he was wrestled over to the flaying table by several escort-beings apparently constituted entirely *of fire,* such that, when they grabbed him (their searing touch instantaneously burning away his funeral suit), his pain was so great that he could no longer struggle or move at all, except his head turned briefly in my direction, and his eyes (horror-filled) met mine.

The diamond doors crashed shut.

It was my turn.

How did you live? asked the being on the right.

Seen from this close, he took on the aspect of Mr. Prindle from my old school, whose thin lips used to purse sadistically as he flogged us precisely.

Tell it truthfully, the other warned, in the voice of my sodden Uncle Gene (always so harsh with me, who had once, drunk, hurled me down the stairs of the granary), as from either side they bumped their heads to mine.

I endeavored to let them fully in; to hold nothing back, to hide nothing; to provide as true an accounting of my life as was in my power.

They recoiled even more fiercely than before, and the smaller versions of themselves rushed forward with even larger gray stone pots, into which my yellow-footed judges began to vomit spasmodically.

I looked at the Christ-emissary.

His eyes were cast down.

May we confirm? said the being on the left. From the right came the feces-mirror. From the left the scale.

Quick check, the Christ-emissary said.

I turned and ran.

I was not pursued. I do not know why. They could have caught me easily. Of course they could! As I ran, whips of fire flew past my ears, and I understood, from whispers delivered therefrom, the whips to be saying:

Tell no one about this.

Or it will be worse upon your return.

(Upon my *return*? I thought, and a splinter of terror entered my heart, and is lodged there still.)

I ran for days, weeks, months, back up the trail, until one night, stopping to rest, I fell asleep and woke up . . . here.

Here again.

And grateful, so deeply grateful.

I have been here since and have, as instructed, refrained from speaking of any of this, to anyone.

What would be the point? For any of us *here*, it is too late for any alteration of course. All is done. We are shades, immaterial, and since that judgment pertains to what we did (or did not do) in that previous (material) realm, correction is now forever beyond our means. Our work there is finished; we only await payment.

I have thought long and hard on what might have caused me to merit that terrible punishment.

I do not know.

I did not kill, steal, abuse, deceive; was not an adulterer, always tried to be charitable and just; believed in God and endeavored, at all times, to the best of my ability, to live according to His will.

And yet was damned.

Was it my (occasional) period of doubt? Was it that I sometimes lusted? Was it my pride, when I had resisted my lust? Was it the timidity I showed by *not* following my lust? Was it that I wasted my life fulfilling outward forms? Did I, in my familial affairs, commit some indiscretion, oversight, or failing that now escapes my memory? Was it my hubris (utter!) in believing that I, living *there* (confined by mind and body), could possibly imagine what was going to occur *here*? Was it some sin so far beyond my ability to comprehend it that even now I remain unaware of it, ready to commit it again?

I do not know.

Many times I have been tempted to blurt out the truth to Mr. Bevins and Mr. Vollman: *A terrible judgment awaits you*, I long to say. *Staying here, you merely delay. You are dead, and shall never regain that previous place. At daybreak, when you must return to your bodies, have you not noticed their disgusting states? Do you really believe those hideous wrecks capable of bearing you anywhere ever again? And what is more* (I would say, if permitted): *you shall not be allowed to linger here forever. None of us shall. We are in rebellion against the will of our Lord, and in time must be broken, and go.*

But, as instructed, I have remained silent.

This is perhaps the worst of my torments: I may not tell the truth. I may speak, but never about the essential thing. Bevins and Vollman consider me an arrogant hectoring pedant, a droning old man; they roll their eyes when I offer counsel, but little do they know: my counsel is infused with bitter and excellent experience.

And so I cower and stall, hiding here, knowing all the while (most dreadful) that, though I remain ignorant of what sin I committed, my ledger stands just as it did on that awful day. I have done nothing to improve it since. For there is nothing *to* do, in this place where no action can matter.

Terrible.

Most terrible.

Is it possible that another person's experience might differ from mine? That he might proceed to some other place? And have there some entirely divergent experience? Is it possible, that is, that what I saw was only a figment of my mind, my beliefs, my hopes, my secret fears?

No.

It was real.

As real as the trees now swaying above me; as real as the pale gravel trail below; as real as the fading, webbed boy breathing shallowly at my feet, banded down snugly across his chest like a captive of the wild Indians, a victim of my negligence (lost in the above recollections, I had long ago ceased laboring on his behalf); as real as Mr. Vollman and Mr. Bevins, who now came run-skimming up the path, looking happier (far happier) than I had ever before seen them.

We did it! said Vollman. We actually did it!

It was us! said Bevins.

We entered and persuaded the fellow! said Vollman.

Propelled by mutual joy, they vaulted in tandem on to the roof.

And indeed: miracle of miracles, they had brought the gentleman back. He entered the clearing below us, holding a lock: the lock to the door of the white stone home, which (though bent in grief) he was tossing up and down in one hand, like an apple.

The moon shone down brightly, allowing me a first good look at his face.

And what a face it was.

the reverend everly thomas

LXII.

The nose heavy and somewhat Roman, the cheeks thin and furrowed, the skin bronzed, the lips full, the mouth wide.

In "Personal Recollections of
Abraham Lincoln and the Civil War,"
by James R. Gilmore.

His eyes dark grey, clear, very expressive, and varying with every mood.

In "The Life of Abraham Lincoln,"
by Isaac N. Arnold.

His eyes were bright, keen, and a luminous gray color.

In "Lincoln's Photographs: A Complete
Album," by Lloyd Ostendorf, account of
Martin P. S. Rindlaub.

Gray-brown eyes sunken under thick eyebrows, and as though encircled by deep and dark wrinkles.

In "Personal Recollections of Mr. Lincoln,"
by the Marquis de Chambrun.

His eyes were a bluish-brown.

In "Herndon's Informants," edited by
Douglas L. Wilson and Rodney O. Davis,
account of Robert Wilson.

His eyes were blueish-gray in color—always in deep shadow, however, from the upper lids, which were unusually heavy.

In "Six Months in the White House:
The Story of a Picture," by F. B. Carpenter.

Kind blue eyes, over which the lids half dropped.

In "With Lincoln from Washington to Richmond in 1865," by John S. Barnes.

I would say, that the eyes of Prest. Lincoln, were of blueish-grey or rather greyish-blue; for, without being *positive,* the blue ray was always visible.

In papers of Ruth Painter Randall, account of Edward Dalton Marchant.

The saddest eyes of any human being that I have ever seen.

In "Lincoln's Melancholy: How Depression Challenged a President and Fueled His Greatness," by Joshua Wolf Shenk, account of John Widmer.

None of his pictures do him the slightest justice.

In the Utica "Herald."

The pictures we see of him only half represent him.

Shenk, op. cit., account of Orlando B. Ficklin.

In repose, it was the saddest face I ever knew. There were days when I could scarcely look at it without crying.

Carpenter, op. cit.

But when he smiled or laughed . . .

Ostendorf, op. cit., account of James Miner.

It brightened, like a lit lantern, when animated.

In "Lincoln the Man," by Donn Piatt, account of a journalist.

There were more differences between Lincoln dull & Lincoln animated, in facial expression, than I ever saw in any other human being.

In Wilson and Davis, op. cit.,
account of Horace White.

His hair was dark brown, without any tendency to baldness.

In "The True Story of Mary,
Wife of Lincoln," by Katherine Helm,
account of Senator James Harlan.

His hair was black, still unmixed with gray.

In "Chiefly About War Matters,"
by Nathaniel Hawthorne.

His hair, well silvered, though the brown then predominated; his beard was more whitened.

In "A Wisconsin Woman's Picture of
President Lincoln," by Cordelia A. P.
Harvey, in "The Wisconsin Magazine of
History."

His smile was something most lovely.

In "A Recollection of the Civil War: With
the Leaders at Washington and in the Field
in the Sixties," by Charles A. Dana.

His ears were large and malformed.

In "Abraham Lincoln: A Medical
Appraisal," by Abraham M. Gordon.

When he was in a good humour I always expected him to flap with them like a good-natured elephant.

In "Ten Years of My Life," by Princess Felix
Salm-Salm.

His nose was not relatively oversized, but it looked large because of his thin face.

In "Abraham Lincoln's Philosophy of Common Sense," by Edward J. Kempf.

His nose is rather long but he is rather *long* himself, so it is a Necessity to keep the proportion complete.

In "Mary Lincoln: Biography of a Marriage," by Ruth Painter Randall, account of a soldier.

His Way of Laughing two was rearly funney and Such awkward Jestures belonged to No other Man they actracted Universal attention from the old Sedate down to the School Boy then in a few Minnets he was as Calm & thoughtful as a Judge on the Bench.

Wilson and Davis, op. cit., account of Abner Ellis.

I thought him about the ugliest man I had ever seen.

In Francis F. Browne, "The Every-Day Life of Abraham Lincoln: A Biography of the Great American President from an Entirely New Standpoint, with Fresh and Invaluable Material," account of Rev. George C. Noyes.

The first time I saw Mr. Lincoln I thought him the homeliest man I had ever seen.

In "My Day and Generation," by Clark E. Carr.

The ugliest man I have ever put my eyes on.

In "The Photographs of Abraham Lincoln," by Frederick Hill Meserve and Carl Sandburg, account of Colonel Theodore Lyman.

The homeliest man I ever saw.

Piatt, op. cit.

Not only is the ugliest man I ever saw, but the most uncouth and gawky in his manners and appearance.

In "Lincoln," by David Herbert Donald, account of a soldier.

He was never handsome, indeed, but he grew more and more cadaverous and ungainly month by month.

In "Lincoln's Washington: Recollections of a Journalist Who Knew Everybody," by W. A. Croffut.

After you have been five minutes in his company you cease to think that he is either homely or awkward.

In the Utica "Herald."

Regarding a face & carriage so uniquely arranged by Nature, one's opinion of it seemed to depend more than usual on the predisposition of the Observer.

In "Letters of Sam Hume," edited by Crystal Barnes.

He never appeared ugly to me, for his face, beaming with boundless kindness and benevolence towards mankind, had the stamp of intellectual beauty.

Salm-Salm, op. cit.

The good humor, generosity, and intellect beaming from it, makes the eye love to linger there until you almost fancy him good-looking.

In "Way-Side Glimpses, North and South," by Lillian Foster.

The neighbors told me that I would find that Mr. Lincoln was an ugly man, when he is really the handsomest man I ever saw in my life.

In "Reminiscences of Abraham Lincoln by Distinguished Men of His Time," by Allen Thorndike Rice.

I never saw a more thoughtful face, I never saw a more dignified face.

Rice, op. cit., account of David Locke.

Oh, the pathos of it!—haggard, drawn into fixed lines of unutterable sadness, with a look of loneliness, as of a soul whose depth of sorrow and bitterness no human sympathy could ever reach. The impression I carried away was that I had seen, not so much the President of the United States, as the saddest man in the world.

Browne, op. cit.

LXIII.

Each motion seeming to require a terrible effort on his part, Mr. Lincoln took hold of the chain and hung the lock upon it.

roger bevins iii

The door being ajar, however, and his boy's sick-form within, it seemed he could not resist making one final entry.

the reverend everly thomas

Vaulting down from the roof, we followed him in.

hans vollman

The sick-form's proximity seeming to jar Mr. Lincoln loose from some prior resolution, he slid the box out of the wall-slot and lowered it to the floor.

the reverend everly thomas

This, it seemed, was as far as he meant to go.

roger bevins iii

(He had not meant even to go this far.)

the reverend everly thomas

Except then he knelt.

hans vollman

Kneeling there, it seemed he could not resist opening the box one last time.

the reverend everly thomas

He opened it; looked in; sighed.

roger bevins iii

Reached in, tenderly rearranged the forelock.

hans vollman

Made a slight adjustment to the pale crossed hands.

roger bevins iii

The lad cried out from the roof.

hans vollman

We had forgotten about him entirely.

roger bevins iii

I stepped out, vaulted back up, worked for some time to get him free. He was in rough shape: stunned speechless, banded-down good.

Then it occurred to me: if I could not pull him *up,* perhaps he could be pushed *down*.

And I was quite right: he had not been impaired at all yet beneath his back.

Working my hands in through the pulpy, still-forming carapace until I felt his chest, I gave him a good shove there, and down he went, with a cry of pain, *through* the roof, into the white stone home.

hans vollman

The boy came through the ceiling and landed on the floor beside his father.

Followed closely by Mr. Vollman.

roger bevins iii

Who, from his knees, urged the boy forward.

Go in, listen well, he said. You may learn something useful.

We have recently heard your father express a certain wish, said Mr. Bevins.

Of where he hopes you are, said Mr. Vollman.

In *some bright place,* said Mr. Bevins.

Free of suffering, said Mr. Vollman.

Resplendent in a new mode of being, said Mr. Bevins.

Go in, said Mr. Vollman.

Be thus guided, said Mr. Bevins. See what he would have you do.

the reverend everly thomas

The lad got weakly to his feet.

hans vollman

Greatly compromised by his affliction.

roger bevins iii

In the gait of an old man, he hobbled toward his father.

the reverend everly thomas

He had not entered the man intentionally before, but inadvertently.

hans vollman

And seemed reluctant to do so now.

roger bevins iii

LXIV.

All this time the crowd had been reassembling around the white stone home.

roger bevins iii

Word of this second visitation having spread rapidly.

the reverend everly thomas

With more individuals arriving every moment.

hans vollman

Such was their eagerness to be in attendance at this extraordinary event.

roger bevins iii

All craved the slightest participation in the transformative moment that must be imminent.

hans vollman

They had abandoned any pretext of speaking one at a time, many calling out desperately from where they stood, others darting brazenly up to the open door to shout their story in.

roger bevins iii

The result was cacophony.

the reverend everly thomas

LXV.

It was me started that fire.

andy thorne

I steal every chanse I git.

janice p. dwightson

I give her dimonds and perls and broke the harts of wife and children and sell the house from under us to buy more dimonds and perls but she thows me over for mr hollyfen with his big yellow laughing horseteeth and huge preceding paunch?

robert g. twistings

Sixty acres with a good return & a penful of hog & thirty head cattle & six fine horses & a cobbled stone house snug as a cradle in winter & a fine wife who looks adoringly at me & three fine boys who hang on my every word & a fine orchard giving pears apples plums peaches & still Father don't care for me?

lance durning

One thing I dont like is I am dumb! Everyone treats me like I am dumb all my life. And I am! Dumb. Even sewing for me is a hard one. My aunt who raised me sat hours showing me sewing. Do it like this, hon, she would say. And I would. Once. Then next time I needed to do it that way I would just sit there, needle raised. And auntie would say lord child this is the nine-millionth time I am showing you this. Whatever it was. See, now I cant remember! What it was. What auntie showed me that I forgot. When a young man come a-courting he would say something such as about the guv'ment and I would say, oh, yes, the guv'ment, my aunts teaching me to sew. And his face'd go blank. Who would want to hold or love one so dull. Unless she is fair. Which I am not. Just plain. Soon I am too old for the young men to come and be bored and that is that. And my teeth go yellow and some fall out. But even when you are a solitary older lady it is no treat to be dumb. Always at a party or so on you are left to sit by the fire, smiling as if happy, knowing none desire to speak with you.

miss tamara doolittle

Lugged seventy-pound pipe-lengths up Swatt Hill—Come home hands torn to hell & bleeding—Rolled gravel nineteen hours straight—& look how I am rewarded—Edna & girls shuffling in and out, gowns stained attending me—Always worked hard, worked cheerful—& once I am better will get right back at it—Only, my left boot needs resoled—& need to collect what Dougherty owes me—Edna knows not of it—& it will go uncollected I fear—It is much needed just now—As I cannot work—If you could kindly inform Edna—So she may collect—It is much needed just now—As I am ill & abed and of little use to them.

tobin "badger" muller

Mr. Johns Melburn did take me to a remote part of the manse and touch me in an evil way. I was just a boy. And he an eminence. Not a word of protest did I (could I) speak. Ever. To anyone. I should like to speak of it now. I should like to speak of it and speak of—

vesper johannes

Mr. DeCroix and Professor Bloomer came blundering up, shouldering Mr. Johannes rudely aside, lurching bumpily up into the doorway, conjoined at the hip from their many years of mutual flattery.

the reverend everly thomas

In my time, I made many discoveries previously unknown in the scientific pantheon, for which I was never properly credited. Have I mentioned how dull my peers were? My research dwarfed theirs in importance. Yet they believed their research dwarfed mine. I was regarded by them as a minor figure. When I knew very well I was quite major. I produced eighteen distinct brilliant tomes, each breaking entirely new ground on such topics as—

Many apologies.

I find myself temporarily unable to recall my exact area of study.

I do, however, recall that final ignominy, when, after my departure, and before I was propelled here (as I lingered, agitated, in that familiar maple), my house was emptied and my papers lugged into a vacant lot and—

professor edmund bloomer

Don't get worked up, sir.

When you lurch about like that it pains me at our juncture.

lawrence t. decroix

And burned!

My brilliant unpublished tomes were burned.

professor edmund bloomer

There, there. Do you know what became of my pickle factory? Not to change the subject? It stands. Of that, at least, I am proud. Although pickles are no longer made there. It is now some sort of boat-building establishment. And the name of DeCroix Pickles has been all but—

lawrence t. decroix

So unfair! My work, my ground-breaking work, went up in a cloud of—

professor edmund bloomer

I feel that way too, you know, about my factory. It was so vital, in its day. The morning-whistle would sound, and from the surrounding houses would pour my seven hundred loyal—

lawrence t. decroix

Thank you for agreeing it was so unfair. Not many are so keenly discriminating. So intuitively sympathetic. To my work. I believe you would have recognized me for the great man I was. If only we had met! If only you had been the editor of one of the premier scientific journals of my day! You could have published my work. And seen that I got my due. At any rate, I thank you, from the heart, for acknowledging that I was the foremost thinker of my time. I feel some measure of redemption, having been at last recognized as the finest mind of my generation.

professor edmund bloomer

Say, did you ever taste one of my pickles? If you ate a pickle in the Washington area during the early part of the century, the odds are good it was a "DeCroix Ferocious."

lawrence t. decroix

The jars had a red-and-yellow label, as I recall. And upon each, a drawing of a wolverine in a waistcoat?

professor edmund bloomer

Yes! Those were my pickles! Did you think they were good?

lawrence t. decroix

Very good.

professor edmund bloomer

Thank you so much, for saying my pickles were excellent. Thanks for saying that, of all of the pickles being made in the nation at that time, mine were, by far, the best.

lawrence t. decroix

They were like my work: the greatest in the world at that time. Wouldn't you say? Can we agree upon that point?

professor edmund bloomer

I believe we can.

I believe we have.

On many prior occasions.

lawrence t. decroix

I hope that soon you will again remind me of how much you thought of my work. I find it touching that you admire me so. And perhaps, someday soon, I will again remark upon how fine your pickles were, if that would please you. I would be happy to do so. You are worth it. You who are so loyal, and admire me so much.

professor edmund bloomer

Strange, isn't it? To have dedicated one's life to a certain venture, neglecting other aspects of one's life, only to have that venture, in the end, amount to nothing at all, the products of one's labors utterly forgotten?

lawrence t. decroix

Fortunately, that does not pertain to us.

As we have (once again) reminded ourselves: our considerable accomplishments live on!

professor edmund bloomer

The Barons now charged the doorway, bursting between the two men, briefly severing their conjoinment.

hans vollman

Ouch.

professor edmund bloomer

Say, that stings!

lawrence t. decroix

Upon the separation, and again upon the rejoining!

professor edmund bloomer

Sir.

Rev.

eddie baron

We didn't get to finish.

betsy baron

You rushed us off.

Before.

eddie baron

So.

betsy baron

As I was saying:

F—— them! Those f——ing ingrate snakes have no G———ed right to blame us for a f——ing thing until they walk a f——ing mile in our G———ed shoes and neither f——ing one of the little s——heads has walked even a s——ing half-mile in our f——ing shoes.

eddie baron

Maybe we had too many parties. Maybe that's why they never come see us.

betsy baron

Them kids was born a shrunken old lady and a shrunken old man who didn't know the first G———n thing about how to f——ing enjoy! You know another word for "party"? Celebration. You know another word for "celebrate"? Have f——ing fun. Make f——ing merry. So we drank a little f——ing ale! Had some G———n wine!

eddie baron

Touch of opium now and—

betsy baron

We might have sampled that f——ing substance, so as not to offend—who was it? That brought that? Who started that whole—

eddie baron

Benjamin.

betsy baron

Ah, Benjamin, Benjy! Remember that f——ing mustache? Didn't we hold him down that once, at McMurray's, shave him bald?

eddie baron

I once made the beast with Benjy.

betsy baron

Ah, who didn't? Ha ha! No: although I personally never made the f——ing beast with Benjy, as far as I remember, still, there were times when, among the general, ah, hilarity, it got a little f——ing unclear just who was making the G———ed beast with—

eddie baron

Then, from among that multitude, came a tremendous shout—

the reverend everly thomas

An unhappy murmur arose—

roger bevins iii

And many people began shouting, saying, no, no, it was not appropriate, demanding that the "darkies"—

the reverend everly thomas

"Black beasts"—

hans vollman

"Damnable savages"—

roger bevins iii

Return at once, from whence they had come.

the reverend everly thomas

It was a momentous occasion and they must not spoil it.

hans vollman

Let them have their chance, someone cried from the throng. In this place, we are all the same.

Speak for yourself, someone else shouted.

And we heard the sound of blows.

the reverend everly thomas

But several men and women of the sable hue, having boldly followed the Barons over from the mass grave on the other side of the fence—

roger bevins iii

Were not to be dissuaded.

hans vollman

And would, it seemed, have their say.

the reverend everly thomas

LXVI.

I did always try, in all my aspects, to hew to elevation; to dispense therewith, into myself, those higher virtues of which, rendered without, one verily may sag, and, dwelling there in one's misfortune, what avails.

elson farwell

What the f—— is he saying?

eddie baron

Say it more simple, Elson. So they can f——ing follow you.

betsy baron

Born to an unlucky fate, perforce, what attraction if, saddling sad fate unremorsed, I only succumbed, but, rather, was, instead, always happy to have loaded upon me any fulsome burdens, never dismaying those febrile opportunities to better oneself, such as books (which I many minutes stole from, abjectly accruing ample notes, on pages gleaned from Mr. East's discard), to wit: find out and spelunk what was best and most beaming in my soul, such as: clean linens; gentle motions (as in the dance); shimmering forks held high in mid-conversation, while emitting a jolly whinnying laugh.

elson farwell

The sweetest f——er, but talks so G———ed complicated.

eddie baron

His hip, in our pit? Is right against my hip.

betsy baron

His a—— rests right here, against my shoulder.

eddie baron

We don't mind. He's our friend.

betsy baron

He's one of them, but he's still our friend.

eddie baron

Always polite.

betsy baron

Knows his place.

eddie baron

Exeunting myself to those higher latitudes would, I felt, vault to the fore my more shining aspects, and soon enough (ran my hopes), the Easts, heartily discussing my prospects in some room of constant gleam, would decide, thereunto, to *promote* me, to the house, and instantly my suffering, which had gauged, gnarred, and vexed, bechiding with sooth my loftish sensitivities, would be *converted*, and, gladsome shouting amidway, I would obtain that life which, more tender (i.e., less bashing, more kindlike smiles), would, ah . . .

elson farwell

Assuage.

eddie baron

He always forgets "assuage" right there.

betsy baron

Assuage, yes.

Would assuage my previous unhappiness.

elson farwell

Now watch.

betsy baron

Madder he gets, better he talks.

eddie baron

But alas.

As it turned out.

My previous unhappiness was not assuaged.

Far from it.

One day, we were taken out of Washington, to the country, for the fireworks. Falling ill, I stumbled along the trail, and could not get up, and the sun burning down brightly, how I writhed upon the—

Oh.

elson farwell

How you "writhed upon the trail, and yet no one came."

betsy baron

How I writhed upon the trail, and yet no one came. Until finally, the youngest East child, Reginald, passed, and inquired, Elson, are you ill? And I said that I was, very much so. And he said he would send someone back for me at once.

But no one came. Mr. East did not come, Mrs. East did not come, none of the other East children came, not even Mr. Chasterly, our brutal smirking overseer, ever came.

I believe Reginald may have, in all the excitement about the fireworks, forgotten.

Forgotten about me.

Who had known him since his birth.

And lying there it—

Drat.

elson farwell

Lying there it occurred to you "with the force of revelation."

eddie baron

Lying there it occurred to me with the force of revelation, that I (Elson Farwell, best boy, fondest son of my mother) had been sorely tricked, and (colorful rockets now bursting overhead, into such shapes as Old Glory, and a walking chicken, and a green-gold Comet, as if to celebrate the Joke being played upon me, each new explosion eliciting fresh cries of delight from those fat, spoiled East children) I regretted every moment of conciliation and smiling and convivial waiting, and longed with all my heart (there in the dappled tree-moonshade, that, in my final moments, became all shade) that my health might be restored to me, if just for one hour, so that I might correct my grand error, and enstrip myself of all cowering and false-talk and preening diction, and rise up even yet and stride back to those always-happy Easts and club and knife and rend and destroy them and tear down that tent and burn down that house, and thus secure for myself—

Oh.

elson farwell

"A certain modicum of humanity, for only a beast—"

betsy baron

A certain modicum of humanity, yes, for only a beast would endure what I had endured without objection; and not even a beast would conspire to put on the manners of its masters and hope thereby to be rewarded.

But it was too late.

It is too late.

It shall ever be too late.

When my absence was noted next day, they sent Mr. Chasterly back, and he, having found me, did not deem it necessary to bring me home, but contracted with a German, who threw me on a cart with several others—

elson farwell

That d—— Kraut stole half a loaf off my wife.

eddie baron

Nice bread too.

betsy baron

Which is where we first met Elson.

eddie baron

On back of that cart.

betsy baron

And been friends ever since.

eddie baron

Never will I leave here until I have had my revenge.

elson farwell

Well, you're not getting any f——ing revenge, pal.

eddie baron

There's a lesson in what happened to you, Elson.

betsy baron

If you ain't white, don't try to be white.

eddie baron

If I could return to that previous place, I would avenge myself even now.

Bring down the bedroom shelving on the fat head of little Reginald; cause the Mrs. to break her neck upon the stairs; cause the Mr.'s clothes to burst into flame as he sat at her paralytic's bedside; send a pestilence upon that house and kill all the children, even the baby, who I previously very much—

elson farwell

Well, I must say, Elson—and pardon me for interrupting—I did not have any such harsh experiences as you have been describing.

Mr. Conner, and his good wife, and all of their children and grandchildren were like *family* to me. Never was I separated from my own wife or children. We ate well, were never beaten. They had given us a small but attractive yellow cottage. It was a happy arrangement, all things considered. All men labor under some impingements on their freedom; none is absolutely at liberty. I was (I felt, for the most part) living simply an exaggerated version of *any man's life*. I adored my wife and our children, and did what any working man would do: exactly what would benefit them and keep us all living convivially together; i.e., I endeavored to be a good and honorable servant, to people who were, fortunately for us, good and honorable people themselves.

Of course, there was always a moment, just as an order was given, when a small, resistant voice would make itself known in the back of my mind. Then the necessary job was to *ignore* that voice. It was not a defiant or angry voice, particularly, just that little *human* voice, saying, you know: I wish to do what I wish to do, and not what you are telling me to do.

And I must say, that voice was never quite silenced.

Although it did grow rather *quiet* over the years.

But I must not over-complain on this score. I had many free and happy moments. On Wednesday afternoons, for example, when I would be given two free hours to myself. And all day, every third Sunday, if things were not too hectic. Admittedly, my enjoyments during these respites were rather trivial, almost childish: *I will walk over and talk to Red. I will go to the pond and sit a bit. I will take this path, and not that.* And no one could call out, "Thomas, come hither" or "Thomas, if you please, that tray" or "Thomas, that vegetable bed needs tending, fetch Charles and Violet and put them to work, will you, old boy?"

Unless, of course, such an interruption was necessary. In which case, naturally, they might, indeed, interrupt me. Even on a Wednesday afternoon. Or a Sunday. Or late upon any night all. As I was enjoying an intimate moment with my wife. Or was lost in a much-needed sleep. Or was praying. Or on the privy.

And yet, still: I had my moments. My free, uninterrupted, discretionary moments.

Strange, though: it is the memory of *those* moments that bothers me most.

The thought, specifically, that other men enjoyed whole lifetimes comprised of such moments.

thomas havens

How came you to reside in our pit, sir?

elson farwell

I was in town. On an errand. I experienced a pain in my chest, and—

thomas havens

Did they not seek you?

elson farwell

They sought me mightily!

They seek me still, I am sure.

My wife leading the effort, Mr. and Mrs. Conner showing their full support.

It is just—they have not found me yet.

thomas havens

This fellow was crisply shoved aside by a young mulatto woman in a white smock and a blue-trimmed lace bonnet, trembling wildly, of such startling beauty that a low murmur arose among the white supplicants.

roger bevins iii

Go ahead, Litzie. It's now or f——ing never.

betsy baron

****

litzie wright

Silent.

eddie baron

As always.

betsy baron

What the f—— musta been done to her? To shut her up so tight?

eddie baron

Stepping up beside the mulatto came a stout Negro woman of some years, by all appearances a large, outwardly jolly presence in that previous place, who was not jolly at all now, but livid, and scowling; and her feet, worn to nubs, left two trails of blood behind her, and as she placed her hands (also worked to nubs) on the mulatto's hips, in support, she left bloody prints in two places there on the pale smock, as the mulatto continued to thrum and shake.

the reverend everly thomas

****

litzie wright

What was done to her was done to her many times, by many. What was done to her could not be resisted, was not resisted, sometimes was resisted, which resulted, sometimes, in her being sent away to some far worse place, other times in that resistance simply being forcibly overcome (by fist, knee, board-strike, etc.). What was done to her was done and done. Or just done once. What was done to her affected her not at all, affected her very much, drove her to the nervous shakes, drove her to hateful speech, drove her to leap off the Cedar Creek Bridge, drove her to this obstinate silence. What was done to her was done by big men, small men, boss men, men who happened to be passing the field in which she worked, the teen sons of the boss man or of the men who happened to be passing, a trio of men on a bender who spilled out of the house and, just before departing, saw her there chopping wood. What was done to her was done on a regular schedule, like some sort of sinister churchgoing; was done to her at random times; was never done at all, never once, but only constantly threatened: looming and sanctioned; what was done to her was straightforward missionary fucking; what was done to her was anal fucking (when the poor dear had never even heard of such a thing); what was done to her were small sick things (to the accompaniment of harsh words from stunted country men who would never have dreamed of doing such things to a woman of their own race), done to her as if no one else were there, only him, the man doing it, she nothing more than a (warm, silent) wax figure; what was done to her was: whatever anyone wished to do, and even if someone wished only slightly to do something to her, well, one could do it, it could be done, one did it, it was done, it was done and done and—

mrs. francis hodge

Lieutenant Stone (shouting, "Back, SHARDS, get ye back!") double-timed up at the head of a group of burly white men (Petit, Daly, and Burns among them), who brusquely cleared the black supplicants away from the white stone home, pushing at them with fallen tree-limbs held horizontally at chest-height.

roger bevins iii

Cries of outrage sounded forth from the black contingent.

hans vollman

Ah, said Mr. Havens. Here, as there?

mrs. francis hodge

Not so f——ing rough!

eddie baron

We know them. They're all right!

betsy baron

Petit, Burns, and Daly, broad red faces distorted with rage, stepped menacingly toward the Barons, causing that couple to recede meekly into the crowd.

hans vollman

Upon a signal from Lieutenant Stone, the patrol now drove forward, pinning the black contingent against the dreaded iron fence.

the reverend everly thomas

(Which was not particularly dreadful to them.

As it only exerted its noxious effects on those of us who resided within its limits.)

hans vollman

Hence a standoff resulted: Lieutenant Stone and patrol, from nausea, could not advance close enough to drive the black contingent over the fence, and those individuals, having reached the limit of their willingness to submit to such depredations, continued to hold their position on *this* side.

the reverend everly thomas

Meanwhile, dozens of (white) supplicants rushed opportunistically into the space thus cleared before the white stone home, bellowing their stories into the doorway, until it was impossible to discern any individual voice amid the desperate chorus.

hans vollman

LXVII.

Mr. Lincoln heard none of this, of course.
To him it was just a silent crypt in the dead of night.

the reverend everly thomas

Now came the critical moment.

roger bevins iii

Boy and father must interact.

hans vollman

This interaction must enlighten the boy; must permit or encourage him to go.

roger bevins iii

Or all was lost.

the reverend everly thomas

Why do you delay? Mr. Vollman said to the boy.

roger bevins iii

The lad drew a deep breath, prepared, it seemed, to enter, finally, and be instructed.

hans vollman

LXVIII.

Only, then: bad luck.

roger bevins iii

A lantern-light appeared in the darkness.

hans vollman

Mr. Manders.
The nightwatchman.

roger bevins iii

Who approached looking as he always looks when among us: timorous, somewhat bemused by his own timorousness, eager to return to the guardhouse.

the reverend everly thomas

We were fond of Manders, who kept his courage up on these rounds by calling out to us congenially, assuring us that things "out there" were as they had been; i.e., eating, loving, brawling, births, binges, grudges, all still proceeded apace. Some nights he would mention his children—

roger bevins iii

Philip, Mary, Jack.

hans vollman

And tell us how they were doing.

roger bevins iii

We appreciated these reports rather more than might be expected, given the facetious spirit in which they were delivered.

hans vollman

As he came tonight, he called for a "Mr. Lincoln," now and then amending that form of address to "Mr. President."

the reverend everly thomas

Though we were fond of Manders—

hans vollman

His timing was terrible.

the reverend everly thomas

Awful.

roger bevins iii

The worst.

hans vollman

He calls for my father, said the boy, who still stood weakly against the doorside wall.

Your father is President? the Reverend inquired wryly.

He is, the boy said.

Of? the Reverend asked.

The United States, the boy said.

It is true, I said to the Reverend. He is President. Much time has passed. There is a state called *Minnesota*.

We are at war, said Mr. Vollman. At war with ourselves. The cannons are greatly improved.

Soldiers bivouac within the Capitol, I said.

We saw it all, said Mr. Vollman.

When we were there within him, I said.

roger bevins iii

Mr. Manders stepped through the doorway, lantern blazing in that confined space.

hans vollman

What had been dark was now brightly lit; we could discern the nicks and divots in the stone walls and the wrinkles in Mr. Lincoln's coat.

roger bevins iii

The pale sunken features of the lad's sick-form.

hans vollman

As it lay there within the—

the reverend everly thomas

Sick-box.

hans vollman

Ah, Manders said. Here you are. Sir.

Yes, Mr. Lincoln said.

Terribly sorry to intrude, Manders said. I thought—I thought you might require a light. For the walk back.

Getting rather lengthily to his feet, Mr. Lincoln shook Manders's hand.

roger bevins iii

Seeming ill at ease.

hans vollman

Embarrassed, perhaps, to be found here.

the reverend everly thomas

Kneeling in front of his son's sick-box.

hans vollman

Open sick-box.

the reverend everly thomas

Mr. Manders's eyes involuntarily drifted past Mr. Lincoln, to the contents.

hans vollman

Mr. Lincoln inquired as to how, without his light, Mr. Manders would find his way back. Mr. Manders said that, though he preferred the light, being somewhat squeamish, still, he knew this place like the back of his hand. Mr. Lincoln offered that, if Mr. Manders would give him just a moment more, they might return together. Mr. Manders acceded, and stepped outside.

roger bevins iii

A catastrophe.

the reverend everly thomas

They had not interacted at all.

hans vollman

Nothing had yet occurred, that might benefit the boy.

roger bevins iii

Still the lad did not come forward.

hans vollman

But only continued to lean against the wall, frozen by fear.

the reverend everly thomas

But then we saw that it was not fear at all.

The wall behind him had liquefied, and tendrils had come forth, and four or five now encircled his waist: a hideous crawling belt, holding him fast.

roger bevins iii

We needed time, to get him free.

hans vollman

Must somehow delay the gentleman's departure.

the reverend everly thomas

I looked at Mr. Bevins.

He looked at me.

hans vollman

We saw what must be done.

roger bevins iii

We had the power. To persuade.

hans vollman

Had done it, even within the hour.

roger bevins iii

Mr. Bevins was younger, possessed of multiple (very strong) arms; whereas I, naked and constantly interfered with by my massive disability, was not well-suited to the strenuous labor that would be required to free the lad.

So in I went, into Mr. Lincoln, alone.

hans vollman

LXIX.

And Lord the fellow was low.

He was attempting to formulate a goodbye, in some sort of positive spirit, not wishing to enact that final departure in gloom, in case it might be felt, somehow, by the lad (even as he told himself that the lad was now past all feeling); but all within him was sadness, guilt, and regret, and he could find little else. So he lingered, hoping for some comforting notion to arise, upon which he might expand.

But nothing came.

Low, colder than before, and sadder, and when he directed his mind outward, seeking the comfort of his life *out there*, and the encouragement of his future prospects, and the high regard in which he was held, no comfort was forthcoming, but on the contrary: he was not, it seemed, well thought of, or succeeding in much of anything at all.

hans vollman

LXX.

As the dead piled up in unimaginable numbers and sorrow was added to sorrow, a nation that had known little of sacrifice blamed Lincoln for a dithering mismanagement of the war effort.

In "The Unpopular Mr. Lincoln: The Story of America's Most Reviled President," by Larry Tagg.

The Presdt is an idiot.

In "The Civil War Papers of George B. McClellan," edited by Stephen Sears.

Vain, weak, puerile, hypocritical, without manners, without social grace, and as he talks to you, punches his fists under your ribs.

In "The War Years," by Carl Sandburg, account of Sherrard Clemens.

Evidently a person of very inferior cast of character, wholly unequal to the crisis.

In "The Emergence of Lincoln: Prologue to the Civil War, 1859–1861," by Allan Nevins, account of Edward Everett.

His speeches have fallen like a wet blanket here. They put to flight all notions of greatness.

Tagg, op. cit., account of Congressman Charles Francis Adams.

By all odds, the weakest man who has ever been elected.

Clemens, op. cit.

Will go down to posterity as the man who could not read the signs of the times, nor understand the circumstances and interests of his country . . . who had no political aptitude; who plunged his country into a great war without a plan; who failed without excuse, and fell without a friend.

Tagg, op. cit., from the London
"Morning Post."

The people have, for nineteen months, poured out, at your call, sons, brothers, husbands & money.—What is the result?—Do you ever realize that the desolation, sorrow, grief that pervades this country is owing to you?—that the young men who have been maimed, crippled, murdered, & made invalids for life, owe it to your weakness, irresolution, & want of moral courage?

Tagg, op. cit., letter from S. W. Oakey.

The money flows out, tens of thousands of men wait, are rearranged to no purpose, march pointlessly over expensive bridges thrown up for the occasion, march back across the same bridges, which are then torn down. And nothing whatsoever is accomplished.

In "Letters of a Union Fellow,"
by Tobian Clearly.

If you don't Resign we are going to put a spider in your dumpling and play the Devil with you you god or mighty god dam sundde of a bith go to hell and buss my Ass suck my prick and call my Bolics your uncle Dick god dam a fool and goddam Abe Lincoln who would like you goddam you excuse me for using such hard words with you but you need it you are nothing but a goddam Black nigger.

In "Dear Mr. Lincoln,"
edited by Harold Holzer.

If my wife wishes to leave me, may I compel her at arms to stay in our "union"? Especially when she is a fiercer fighter than I, better organized, quite determined to be free of me?

In "Voices of a Divided Land," edited by Baines and Edgar, account of P. Mallon.

Line up the corpses; walk from end to end; look upon each father, husband, brother, son; total up the cost that way, and think (as our military men, quizzed upon this confidentially, all do) that this grim line of ruined futures is only the beginning of the tidal wave of young death that must soon befall us.

In the Allentown "Field-Gazette."

Peace, sir, make peace: the cry of man since at least our Savior's time. Why ignore it now? Blessed are the peacemakers, the Scriptures say, and we must assume the converse also to be true: Cursed are the warmongers, however just they believe their cause.

In the Cleveland "Truth-Sentinel."

We did not & will not Agree to fite for the Neygar, for whom we do not give a wit.

In "Forgotten Voices of the Civil War," edited by J. B. Strait, letter from a New York infantryman to Lincoln.

You have seized the reins, made yourself dictator, established a monolithic new form of government which must dominate over the rights of the individual. Your reign presages a terrible time when all of our liberties shall be lost in favor of the rights of the monolith. The founders look on in dismay.

In "The Villain Lincoln," by R. B. Arnolds, account of Darrel Cumberland.

So we have the dilemma put to us, What to do, when his power must continue two years longer and when the existence of our country may be endangered before he can be replaced by a man of sense. How hard, in order to save the country, to sustain a man who is incompetent.

In "Lincoln Reconsidered," by David Herbert Donald, letter from George Bancroft to Francis Lieber.

If Abe Lincoln should be re-elected for another term of four years of such wretched administration, we hope that a bold hand will be found to plunge the dagger into the tyrant's heart for the public welfare.

In the "La Crosse Democrat."

Old Abe Lincoln

God damn your god damned old Hellfired god damned soul to hell god damn you and goddam your god damned family's god damned hell-fired god damned soul to hell and god damnation god damn them and god damn your god damn friends to hell god damn their god damned souls to damnation god damn them.

Holzer, op. cit.

LXXI.

Well, what of it.

No one who has ever done anything worth doing has gone uncriticized. As regards the matter at hand (as regards him), I am, at least, above any—

Thus thought Mr. Lincoln.

But then his (*our*) eyes shut, in a slow remembering sorrow-wince.

hans vollman

LXXII.

Harsh whispers made the rounds in those dreadful days, intimating that all that would have been needed to spare the boy's life was the basic restraining influence of a parent.

In "The Prairie Torment:
Lincoln's Psychology," by James Spicer.

Willie was so delighted with a little pony, that he insisted on riding it every day. The weather was changeable, and exposure resulted in a severe cold, which deepened into fever.

Keckley, op. cit.

Why, some asked, was a child riding a pony about in the pouring rain, without a coat?

Spicer, op. cit.

Those of us who knew the Lincoln children personally, and saw them running around the White House like a pair of wild savages, will attest to the fact that this was a household in a state of perpetual bedlam, where indiscriminate permission was confused with filial love.

In "Accidental Jehovah: Will, Focus,
and the Great Deed," by Kristen Toles,
account of B. Milbank.

[Lincoln] exercised no government of any kind over his household. His children did much as they pleased. Many of their antics he approved, and he restrained them in nothing. He never reproved them or gave them a fatherly frown.

In "Life of Lincoln," by
William H. Herndon and Jesse W. Weik.

He always said "It [is my] pleasure that my children are free—happy & unrestrained by parental tyranny. Love is the chain whereby to Lock a child to its parents."

In "Herndon's Informants," edited by
Douglas L. Wilson and Rodney O. Davis,
account of Mary Lincoln.

These children would take down the books—Empty ash buckets—coal ashes—inkstand—papers—gold pens—letters &c. &c in a pile and then dance on the pile. Lincoln would say nothing, so abstracted was he and so blinded to his children's faults. Had they s——t in Lincoln's hat and rubbed it on his boots, he would have laughed and thought it smart.

In "Herndon on Lincoln: Letters," edited by
Douglas L. Wilson and Rodney O. Davis,
letter to Jesse K. Weik.

They could have raced past him into a shooting match and he would not have glanced up from his work. For Lincoln (all subsequent hagiography aside) was an ambitious man—nearly monomaniacally so.

In "They Knew Him," edited by Leonora
Morehouse, account of Theodore Blasgen.

[Any] man who thinks that Lincoln calmly gathered his robes about him, waiting for the people to call him, has a very erroneous knowledge of Lincoln. He was always calculating, and always planning ahead. His ambition was a little engine that knew no rest.

In "The Inner World of
Abraham Lincoln," by Michael Burlingame,
account of William H. Herndon.

One like myself, who long ago made the decision to put aside worldly aspirations for the gentler pleasures of home and family, and to accept, as part of the bargain, a commensurately less glorious public life, can only imagine the dark cloud that must descend upon one's head at the thought of what *might* have happened, had all of one's attention been, as appropriate, on the essential hearthside matters.

In "Wise Words and Collected Letters from a Grandfather" (unpublished manuscript, edited by Simone Grand, used by permission), by Norman G. Grand.

When a child is lost there is no end to the self-torment a parent may inflict. When we love, and the object of our love is small, weak, and vulnerable, and has looked to us and us alone for protection; and when such protection, for whatever reason, has failed, what consolation (what justification, what defense) may there possibly be?

None.

Doubt will fester as long as we live.

And when one occasion of doubt has been addressed, another and then another will arise in its place.

Milland, op. cit.

LXXIII.

Blame and Guilt are the furies that haunt houses where death takes children like Willie Lincoln; and in this case there was more than enough blame to go around.

Epstein, op. cit.

Critics accused the Lincolns of heartlessness, for planning a party while Willie was ill.

Brighney, op. cit.

In retrospect, the memory of that triumphant evening must have been blotted with anguish.

Leech, op. cit.

Finding that Willie continued to grow worse, Mrs. Lincoln determined to withdraw her cards of invitation and postpone the reception. Mr. Lincoln thought that the cards had better not be withdrawn.

Keckley, op. cit.

Willie was burning with fever on the night of the fifth, as his mother dressed for the party. He drew every breath with difficulty. She could see that his lungs were congested and she was frightened.

Kunhardt and Kunhardt, op. cit.

At least [Lincoln] advised that the doctor be consulted before any steps were taken. Accordingly Dr. Sloan was called in. He pronounced

Willie better, and said that there was every reason for an early recovery.

Keckley, op. cit.

The doctor assured Lincoln that Willie would recover.

In "The President's Hippocrates," by Deborah Chase, M.D., account of Joshua Freewell.

The house swelled with the triumphant swaggering music supplied by the Marine Band, which fell on the boy's feverish mind like the taunts of a healthy playmate.

Sloane, op. cit.

If the party did not hasten the boy's end it must certainly have exacerbated his suffering.

Mays, op. cit.

A cartoon appeared in a Washington rag called the "Gab & Joust," showing Mr. and Mrs. Lincoln throwing back glasses of champagne as the boy (with tiny Xs for his eyes) climbed into an open grave, inquiring, "Father, a Glass Before I Go?"

In "The Rudderless Ship: When Presidents Flounder," by Maureen H. Hedges.

The noise, the revelry, the manic drunken laughter late into the night, the little boy lying there with his high fever, feeling utterly alone, fighting to stave off the presence of the hooded figure near the door!

Spicer, op. cit.

"Father, a Glass Before I Go?"
"Father, a Glass Before I Go?"
"Father, a Glass Before I Go?"

Hedges, op. cit.

The doctor assured Lincoln that Willie would recover.

Chase, op. cit., account of Joshua Freewell.

Lincoln heeded the doctor's advice.

Stragner, op. cit.

Lincoln failed to overrule the doctor.

Spicer, op. cit.

Electing not to err on the side of caution, the President advised that the party proceed.

Hedges, op. cit.

The party went ahead with the President's blessing, the little boy suffering horribly upstairs.

Chase, op. cit., account of Joshua Freewell.

LXXIV.

Outside, an owl shrieked.

I became aware of the smell rising up off *our* suit: linen, sweat, barley.

I had thought not to come here again.

Thus thought Mr. Lincoln.

Yet here I am.

One last look.

And dropped into a country-squat before the sick-box.

His little face again. Little hands. Here they are. Ever will be. Just so. No smile. Ever again. The mouth a tight line. He does not (no) look like he is sleeping. He was an open-mouthed sleeper and many expressions would play across his face as he dreamed and he would sometimes mumble a few silly words.

If there ever really was a Lazarus, there should be nothing preventing the conditions that pertained at that time to pertain here and now.

Then it was quite something: Mr. Lincoln tried to get the sick-form to rise. By making his mind quiet and then opening it up to whatever might exist that he did not know about that might be able to let the (make the) sick-form rise.

Feeling foolish, not truly believing such a thing was even—

Still, it is a vast world and anything might happen.

He stared down at the sick-form, at one finger upon one hand, waiting for the slightest—

Please please please.

But no.

That is superstition.

Will not do.

(Come around, sir, to good sense.)

I was in error when I saw him as fixed and stable and thought I would have him forever. He was never fixed, nor stable, but always just a passing, temporary energy-burst. I had reason to know this. Had he not looked this way at birth, that way at four, another way at seven, been made entirely anew at nine? He had never stayed the same, even instant to instant.

He came out of nothingness, took form, was loved, was always bound to return to nothingness.

Only I did not think it would be so soon.

Or that he would precede us.

Two passing temporarinesses developed feelings for one another.

Two puffs of smoke became mutually fond.

I mistook him for a solidity, and now must pay.

I am not stable and Mary not stable and the very buildings and monuments here not stable and the greater city not stable and the wide world not stable. All alter, are altering, in every instant.

(Are you comforted?)

No.

(It is time.

To go.)

So distracted was I by the intensity of Mr. Lincoln's musings that I had entirely forgotten my purpose.

But recalled it now.

Stay, I thought. It is imperative that you stay. Let Manders go back alone. Sit on the floor now and be comfortable, and we will usher the boy into you, and who knows what positive outcome may result from this reunion, a reunion which both of you so ardently desire.

I then supplied the most precise mental images I could conjure, of him *staying:* sitting; being content to sit; sitting comfortably, finding peace via the process of staying, etc., etc.

Time to go.

Thought Mr. Lincoln.

Rising up a bit on his haunches in a pre-leaving way.

When, toddling along, he went down, I swept him up and kissed away his tears. When none were playing with him in Prester's Lot I came over with an apple and cut it up. For all.

That did the trick.

That and his natural way.

Soon he was bossing and leading.

And now I am to leave him, unhelped, in this awful place?

(You wallow. He is beyond your help. Old Mr. Grasse in Sangamon went to his wife's grave forty days in a row. At first it seemed admirable but before long we were joking about him and his store went to ruin.)

Therefore, resolved:

Resolved: we must, we must now—

(Cause yourself to have such thoughts, however harsh, as will lead you to do what you know to be right. Look.

Look down.

At him.

At it.

What is it? Frankly investigate that question.

Is it him?)

It is not.

(What is it?)

It is that which used to bear him around. The essential thing (that which was borne, that which we loved) is gone. Though this was part of what we loved (we loved the way he, the combination of spark and bearer, looked and walked and skipped and laughed and played the clown), this, this here, is the lesser part of that beloved contraption. Absent that spark, this, this lying here, is merely—

(Think it. Go ahead. Allow yourself to think that word.)

I would rather not.

(It is true. It will help.)

I need not say it, to feel it, and act upon it.

(It is not right to make a fetish of the thing.)

I will go, I am going, I need no further convincing.

(Say it, though, for truth. Say the word rising up in you.)

Oh my little fellow.

(Absent that spark, this lying here, is merely—

Say it.)

Meat.

An unfortunate—

A most unfortunate conclusion.

I tried again, giving it my all:

Stay, I beseeched. He is not beyond your help. Not at all. You may yet do him much good. Indeed, you may be of more help to him now than you ever were in that previous place.

For his eternity hangs in the balance, sir. If he stays, the misery that will overtake him is quite beyond your imagining.

So: Linger, tarry, do not rush off, sit a spell, make yourself at home, dawdle, and, settling in, be thee content.

I implore you.

I had thought this helpful. It is not. I need not look upon it again. When I need to look upon Willie, I will do so in my heart. As is proper. There where he is yet intact and whole. If I could confer with him, I know he would approve; would tell me it is right that I should go, and come back no more. He was such a noble spirit. His heart loved goodness most.

So good. Dear little chap. Always knew the right thing to do. And would urge me to do it. I will do it now. Though it is hard. All gifts are temporary. I unwillingly surrender this one. And thank you for it. God. Or world. Whoever it was gave it to me, I humbly thank you, and pray that I did right by him, and may, as I go ahead, continue to do right by him.

Love, love, I know what you are.

hans vollman

LXXV.

We had succeeded in hacking our way nearly through the waist-belt with our nails and a sharp stone we had found nearby.

the reverend everly thomas

Almost there! I called in to Mr. Vollman.

roger bevins iii

But it was too late.

the reverend everly thomas

Mr. Lincoln closed the sick-box.
(My heart sank.)

roger bevins iii

Lifted the box, carried it back to the wall-slot, slid it in.
(All was lost.)

the reverend everly thomas

And walked out the door.

roger bevins iii

LXXVI.

Into the now-hushed crowd.

the reverend everly thomas

Which parted meekly to let him through.

roger bevins iii

Gone? the boy cried out.

We had him free now. He pushed out from the wall and, staggering a few steps away, sat on the floor.

the reverend everly thomas

Where the tendrils immediately began to take him again.

roger bevins iii

LXXVII.

Come, I said to Mr. Bevins. I, alone, was insufficient. I think we must both try. To stop him.

hans vollman

Reverend, Mr. Bevins said to me. Will you join us? Even one additional mind may make the difference.

Especially a mind as powerful as yours, said Mr. Vollman.

Many years ago, I had joined my friends in performing *l'occupation* upon an estranged young couple who had snuck into this place after-hours. We had, on that occasion, caused the young people to fornicate. And become re-engaged. A year or so after that reconciliation, the young husband returned to this place, seeking the site of that assignation. Curious, we performed *l'occupation* again, and found that those causes for dissension which had initially sundered their engagement had, in the fecund climate of marriage, grown and festered, leading, recently, to the self-destruction, by poison, of his young wife.

Our interference on that occasion had, it must be said, left blood on our hands.

I had vowed, there and then, never again to participate in that practice.

But my affection for the boy, and my sense that my earlier inattention had compromised him, caused me now to renounce that oath, and join my friends.

the reverend everly thomas

Dashing out of the white stone home, run-skimming as fast as we could, the three of us closed rapidly on Mr. Lincoln.

roger bevins iii

Then leapt.

hans vollman

Into the President.

roger bevins iii

The crowd swarming around us.

hans vollman

Several bolder individuals, inspired by our example, also made to enter.

the reverend everly thomas

By first taking exploratory runs through the President, or brushing glancingly against him, or darting into and then out of him, as a loon might break the surface of a lake to seize a fish.

hans vollman

Mr. Cohoes, outspoken former boilermaker, matching Mr. Lincoln's pace, strolled into him from behind, and stayed there, moving identically within him, stride for stride.

roger bevins iii

Nothing to it! Cohoes said, his voice gone high-pitched with the audacity of the act.

the reverend everly thomas

All were now emboldened.

hans vollman

Soon it became a general movement.

roger bevins iii

No one wishing to be excluded.

hans vollman

Many individuals encroaching upon one another—

the reverend everly thomas

Entering one another—

hans vollman

Becoming multiply conjoined—

roger bevins iii

Shrinking down as necessary—

hans vollman

So that all might be accommodated.

roger bevins iii

Mrs. Crawford entered, being groped as usual by Mr. Longstreet.

hans vollman

The stabbed Mr. Boise entered; Andy Thorne entered; Mr. Twistings entered, as did Mr. Durning.

roger bevins iii

The Negro contingent, having broken free of Lieutenant Stone and his patrol, came therein; Stone and patrol, offended by the notion of proximity to those persons, declined to follow.

the reverend everly thomas

The Barons were now therein; Miss Doolittle, Mr. Johannes, Mr. Bark, and Tobin "Badger" Muller were therein.

roger bevins iii

Along with many others.

hans vollman

Too many to enumerate.

the reverend everly thomas

So many wills, memories, complaints, desires, so much raw life-force.

roger bevins iii

It occurred to us now (as Manders, lantern held high, preceded the President into a grove of trees) that we might *harness* that mass power, to serve our purpose.

hans vollman

What Mr. Vollman had been unable to accomplish alone—

roger bevins iii

Perhaps all of us, working as one, might.

the reverend everly thomas

And so, as the lantern-light fell out aslant before us, I requested that everyone therein, all at once, exhort Mr. Lincoln *to stop*.

hans vollman

(We would *stop* him first, and, if successful, endeavor to *send him back*.)

the reverend everly thomas

All willingly agreed.

roger bevins iii

Flattered to be asked to do anything at all, or participate in the slightest thing.

the reverend everly thomas

Stop! I thought, and that multitude joined me, each expressing that impulse in his or her own manner.

roger bevins iii

Pause, cease, self-interrupt.

hans vollman

Desist, halt, discontinue all forward motion.
And so on.

the reverend everly thomas

What a pleasure. What a pleasure it was, being in there. Together. United in common purpose. In there together, yet also within one another, thereby receiving glimpses of one another's minds, and glimpses, also, of Mr. Lincoln's mind. How good it felt, doing this together!

roger bevins iii

We thought.

hans vollman

We all thought.

the reverend everly thomas

As one. Simultaneously.

hans vollman

One mass-mind, united in positive intention.

roger bevins iii

All selfish concerns (of staying, thriving, preserving one's strength) momentarily set aside.

the reverend everly thomas

What a refreshment.

hans vollman

To be free of all of that.

roger bevins iii

We were normally so alone.
Fighting to stay.
Afraid to err.

hans vollman

We had not always been so solitary. Why, back in that previous place—

the reverend everly thomas

We now recalled—

hans vollman

All instantaneously recollected—

the reverend everly thomas

Suddenly, I *remembered:* the showing up at church, the sending of flowers, the baking of cakes to be brought over by Teddie, the arm around the shoulder, the donning of black, the waiting at the hospital for hours.

roger bevins iii

Leverworth giving Burmeister a kind word at the lowest moment of the bank scandal; Furbach drawing out his purse to donate generously to Dr. Pearl, for there had been a fire in the West District.

hans vollman

The handholding group of us wading into the surf to search for poor drowned Chauncey; the sound of coins falling into the canvas bag crudely labeled Our Poor; a group of us on our knees weeding the churchyard at dusk; the clanking of the huge green soup pot as my deacon and I lugged it out to those wretched women of the evening in the Sheep's Grove.

the reverend everly thomas

The happy mob of us children gathered about a tremendous vat of boiling chocolate, and dear Miss Bent, stirring it, making fond noises at us, as if we were kittens.

roger bevins iii

My God, what a thing! To find oneself thus expanded!

hans vollman

How had we forgotten? All of these happy occasions?

the reverend everly thomas

To stay, one must deeply and continuously dwell upon one's primary reason for staying; even to the exclusion of all else.

roger bevins iii

One must be constantly looking for opportunities to tell one's story.

hans vollman

(If not *permitted* to tell it, one must think it and think it.)

the reverend everly thomas

But this had cost us, we now saw.
We had forgotten so much, of all else we had been and known.

roger bevins iii

But now, through this serendipitous mass co-habitation—

the reverend everly thomas

We found ourselves (like flowers from which placed rocks had just been removed) being restored somewhat to our natural fullness.

roger bevins iii

As it were.

hans vollman

It felt good.

the reverend everly thomas

It did.

hans vollman

Very good.

roger bevins iii

And seemed to be doing us good as well.

the reverend everly thomas

Looking over, I found Mr. Vollman suddenly *clad*, his member shrunk down to normal size. His clothes were, it is true, decidedly *scruffy* (printer's apron, ink-dotted shoes, mismatched socks) but nevertheless: a miracle.

roger bevins iii

Becoming aware of Mr. Bevins staring at me, I glanced over and found him no longer a difficult-to-look-at clustering of eyes, noses, hands, et al.—but a handsome young man, of eager and pleasing countenance: two eyes, one nose, two hands, ruddy cheeks, a beautiful head of black hair in that vicinity so previously overgrown with eyeballs as to make hair a redundancy.

An appealing young fellow, in other words, with the proper number of everything.

hans vollman

Excuse me, the Reverend said somewhat shyly. May I ask? How do I look?

Very well, I said. Quite at ease.

Not afraid at all, said Mr. Vollman.

Eyebrows at the proper height, I said. Eyes not overly wide.

Hair no longer sticking straight up, said Mr. Vollman.

Mouth no longer an O, I said.

roger bevins iii

And we were not the only beneficiaries of this happy blessing.

the reverend everly thomas

For reasons unknown to us, Tim Midden had always gone about dogged by a larger version of himself, that was constantly leaning over to whisper discouragement to him; this behemoth was now gone.

hans vollman

Mr. DeCroix and Professor Bloomer had become unconjoined and, no matter how close together they walked, did not rejoin.

roger bevins iii

Mr. Tadmill, disgraced clerk, who had misfiled an important document, causing the collapse of his firm, and had thereafter been unable to find other employment, and had begun to drink, and lost his home, and saw his wife placed into a sick-box due to excessive worry and their children dispersed to various orphanages in light of his ever-increasing dissipation, usually presented nearly bent to the ground with regret, shaped like one half of a set of parentheses topped with a sad sprig of white hair, quaking all over, moving with extreme caution, terrified of making even the smallest mistake.

But now we saw a spry young tow-headed fellow just embarking upon a new position, full of high hopes, flower in his lapel.

the reverend everly thomas

Mr. Longstreet discontinued his groping, burst into tears, begged Mrs. Crawford's forgiveness.

roger bevins iii

(It is just that I am lonely, dear girl.)

sam "smooth-boy" longstreet

(If you wish, I can tell you the names of some of our wildwoods flowers.)

mrs. elizabeth crawford

(It would be a pleasure to hear them.)

sam "smooth-boy" longstreet

Verna Blow and her mother, Ella, who normally manifested as virtually identical hags (though both had died in childbirth, and had therefore never grown old in that previous place), now appeared (each pushing a baby carriage) youthful again, utterly ravishing.

hans vollman

Poor multiply raped Litzie became capable of speech, her first utterance consisting of words of thanks to Mrs. Hodge for speaking for her, during all of those mute and lonely years.

elson farwell

Mrs. Hodge, dear woman, accepted Litzie's thanks with a dull nod, looking down in wonder at her own newly restored hands and feet.

thomas havens

Those miraculous transformations among us notwithstanding, Mr. Lincoln was not stopping.

roger bevins iii

At all.

hans vollman

On the contrary.

the reverend everly thomas

Seemed to be walking faster than ever.

roger bevins iii

Intent on leaving this place as quickly as possible.

hans vollman

Ah, me, mumbled Verna Blow, whose restored youthful beauty struck me as wonderful, even in that moment of colossal defeat.

roger bevins iii

LXXVIII.

I called for the Bachelors, who came at once, and hovered above, dropping down (in their dear and naive mode of attentiveness) tiny graduation caps, as I explained that we were in a desperate situation, and asked them to go forth across the premises and bring back whatever additional help they could enlist.

How exactly would we say it? inquired Mr. Kane.

We aren't exactly "kings of words"! said Mr. Fuller.

Tell them that we work to save a boy, Mr. Vollman said. Whose only sin is that he is a child, and the architect of this place has, for reasons we cannot know, deemed that, to be a child and to love one's life enough to desire to stay here is, in this place, a terrible sin, worthy of the most severe punishment.

Tell them we are tired of being nothing, and doing nothing, and mattering not at all to anyone, and living in a state of constant fear, the Reverend said.

Not sure we can remember all that, said Mr. Kane.

Sounds like quite a commitment, said Mr. Fuller.

We'll defer to Mr. Lippert, said Mr. Kane. As he is senior among us.

roger bevins iii

Although, in Truth, we Three were all of the same age, each of us having come to this Place in the midst of his twenty-eighth Year (unloved & unwed, as of yet), I was indeed, *technically,* the Ranking member of our little Party, having been here first (& Lonely) for near nine years, at which time I had been Joined by Mr. Kane (deliver'd here by the untimely occasion of an Indian Lance piercing him in the buttocks), after which Mr. Kane and I became an Inseparable Duo, for nearly eleven years, at which time that Young Cub, Mr. Fuller, having made an ill-advised drunken Leap off a Delaware silo, completed our Trio.

And it seemed to me, having given it my Consideration, that it was not in our best Interest to get involved, for this Affair had nothing to do with us, & might Threaten our very Freedom, & burden us with Noxious Obligations, & constrain us in our Endeavor of doing, at all times, Exactly what we Liked, & might even exert a Deleterious Effect upon our ability to Stay.

Terribly sorry, I shouted down. We do not wish to, and, therefore, shall not!

stanley "perfesser" lippert

The hats the Bachelors sent down now were bowlers: black, somber, funereal, as if, for all their habitual levity, they understood the gravity of the moment and, though they had no intention of lingering, regretted not being more helpful.

the reverend everly thomas

But their sadness did not last long.

hans vollman

They sought love (or so they told themselves); and hence must always be in motion: hopeful, jocular, animated, continually looking and seeking.

roger bevins iii

Seeking any new arrival, or old arrival overlooked, whose unprecedented loveliness might justify the forfeiture of their prized freedom.

the reverend everly thomas

So off they went.

hans vollman

"Perfesser" Lippert in the lead, we embarked on a merry chase across the premises.

gene "rascal" kane

Flying low over hills and paths, proceeding at speed through sick-houses and sheds and trees and even a deer of that other realm.

jack "malarkey" fuller

Who, startled at our nearly simultaneous entry and exit, reared up, as if bee-stung.

gene "rascal" kane

LXXIX.

In discouragement, individuals began to abandon Mr. Lincoln.

roger bevins iii

Bundling themselves into fetal balls, and tumbling out.

hans vollman

Vaulting out, with gymnastic flair.

roger bevins iii

Or simply slowing slightly, allowing the President to walk out of them.

hans vollman

Each fell prostrate upon the trail, moaning with disappointment.

the reverend everly thomas

It had all been a flim-flam.

roger bevins iii

A chimera.

the reverend everly thomas

Mere wishful thinking.

roger bevins iii

Finally, passing J. L. Bagg, *He Lives Now Forever in the Light*, even we three dropped out.

hans vollman

First Bevins, then Vollman, then I.

the reverend everly thomas

Falling out in sequence along the path, near the Muir memorial.

hans vollman

(A cluster of angels, fussing over twin boys in sailor garb, who lay side by side on a slab.)

roger bevins iii

(Felix and Leroy Muir.
Perished at Sea.)

the reverend everly thomas

(It was not well-done. It appeared the angels meant to operate on the young sailors. But were confused as to how to begin.)

hans vollman

(Also, for some reason, a pair of oars lay upon the operating table.)

roger bevins iii

Only then did we remember the lad, and what he must now be enduring.

hans vollman

And roused ourselves, despite our weariness, and started back.

roger bevins iii

LXXX.

And though that mass co-habitation had jarred much loose from me (a nagging, hazy mental cloud of details from my life now hung about me: names, faces, mysterious foyers, the smells of long-ago meals; carpet patterns from I knew not what house, distinctive pieces of cutlery, a toy horse with one ear missing, the realization that my wife's name had been *Emily*), it had not delivered the essential truth I sought, as to why I had been damned. I halted on the trail, lagging behind, desperate to bring that cloud into focus and recall who I had been, and what evil I had done, but was not successful in this, and then had to hurry to catch my friends up.

the reverend everly thomas

LXXXI.

The lad lay collapsed on the floor of the white stone home, cocooned to the neck in a carapace that appeared fully concretized.

hans vollman

The putrid smell of wild onions pervaded that vicinity, progressing, in its density, toward a different, more sinister odor, for which there is no name.

the reverend everly thomas

He lay gazing up at us, dull-eyed, acquiescent.

roger bevins iii

It was over.

the reverend everly thomas

The lad must take his medicine.

hans vollman

We gathered around to say goodbye.

roger bevins iii

Imagine our surprise, then, when a woman's voice rang out, offering a parley, suggesting that "HE" would have no objection if we wished to transport the boy back up to the roof, so that he might serve out his (infinite) interment there.

the reverend everly thomas

Mind you, none of this is by our choice, said a bass voice, with a slight lisp. We are compelled.

roger bevins iii

These voices seemed to be emanating from the carapace itself.

hans vollman

Which seemed comprised of *people*. People like us. Like we had been. Former people, somehow shrunken and injected into the very fabric of that structure. Thousands of writhing tiny bodies, none bigger than a mustard seed, twisting minuscule faces up at us.

the reverend everly thomas

Who were they? Who had they been? How had they come to be so "compelled"?

roger bevins iii

We won't discuss that, said the woman's voice. Will not discuss that.

Mistakes were made, said the bass voice.

hans vollman

My advice? said a third, and British, voice. Do not massacre an entire regiment of your enemy.

Never conspire with your lover to dispose of a living baby, said the bass lisper.

roger bevins iii

Rather than murdering your loved one with poison, resolve to endure him, said the woman.

the reverend everly thomas

Sexual congress with children is not permitted, said the voice of an old man, from Vermont, judging by his accent.

hans vollman

As each spoke, the associated face bloomed up out of the carapace for the briefest of instants, bearing upon it a look of agony and aggrievement.

the reverend everly thomas

We had seen many strange things here.

roger bevins iii

But this was the strangest yet.

hans vollman

Are you—are you in Hell? asked the Reverend.

Not the worst one, said the British fellow.

Are not compelled to bash our skulls against a series of clustered screw-drivers at least, said the woman.

Are not being sodomized by a flaming bull, said the bass lisper.

roger bevins iii

Whatever my sin, it must, I felt (I prayed), be small, compared to the sins of *these*. And yet, I was of their ilk. Was I not? When I went, it seemed, it would be to join them.

As I had many times preached, our Lord is a fearsome Lord, and mysterious, and will not be predicted, but judges as He sees fit, and we are but as lambs to Him, whom He regards with neither affection nor malice; some go to the slaughter, while others are released to the meadow, by His whim, according to a standard we are too lowly to discern.

It is only for us to *accept;* accept His judgment, and our punishment.

But, as applied to me, this teaching did not satisfy.

And oh, I was sick, sick at heart.

the reverend everly thomas

What will it be then? said the Brit. In here? Or on the roof?

hans vollman

All eyes turned to the boy.

roger bevins iii

Who blinked twice but said nothing.

hans vollman

Perhaps, Mr. Bevins said. Perhaps you could make an exception.

And from the carapace burst forth the sound of bitter laughter.

He is a fine child, said Mr. Vollman. A fine child, with many—

We have done this to many, many fine children before, said the woman.

Rules are rules, said the Brit.

But why, may I ask, said Mr. Bevins, should there be different rules for children than for the rest of us? It does not seem fair.

From the carapace came outraged rebukes in diverse languages, many of which were utterly strange to us.

Please do not speak to us of fairness, the woman said.

Fairness, bah, said the Vermonter.

Did I murder Elmer? the woman said.

You did, said the Brit.

I did, said the woman. Was I born with just those predispositions and desires that would lead me, after my whole preceding life (during which I had killed exactly no one), to do *just that thing*? I was. Was that *my* doing? Was that *fair*? Did I *ask* to be born licentious, greedy, slightly misanthropic, and to find Elmer so irritating? I did not. But there I was.

And here you are, said the Brit.

Here I am, quite right, she said.

And here I am, said the Vermonter. Did I ask to be born with a desire to have sex with children? I don't remember doing so, there in my mother's womb. Did I fight that urge? Mightily. Well, somewhat mightily. As mightily as I could. As mightily as someone could who had been born with that particular affliction, in that particular measure. Upon leaving that previous place, did I attempt to make that case, to those who arraigned me?

I expect that you did, the woman said.

Of course I did, the Vermonter said indignantly.

And how did they respond? asked the Brit.

Not very well, the Vermonter said.

We have had a great deal of time to think upon these matters, said the woman.

Rather too much, said the Vermonter.

Listen, the bass lisper intoned. At the time Marie and I did away with that baby, we felt ourselves to be working in the service of good. Honestly! We loved one another; the baby was not quite right; was an impediment to our love; its (his) stunted development impeded the natural expression of our love (we could not travel, could not dine out, were rarely given the slightest degree of privacy) and so it seemed (to us, at that time) that to remove the negative influence that was that baby (by dropping him into Furniss Creek) would free us up; to be more loving, and be more fully in the world, and would relieve him of the suffering entailed in being forevermore not quite right; would, that is, free him up from his suffering as well, and maximize the total happiness.

It seemed that way to you, the Brit said.

It did, it truly did, the bass lisper said.

Does it seem that way to you now? the woman asked.

Less so, the bass lisper said sadly.

Then your punishment is having the desired effect, the woman said.

the reverend everly thomas

We were as we were! the bass lisper barked. How could we have been otherwise? Or, being that way, have *done* otherwise? We *were* that way, *at that time*, and had been led to that place, not by any innate evil in ourselves, but by the state of our cognition and our experience up *until that moment*.

By Fate, by Destiny, said the Vermonter.

By the fact that time runs in only one direction, and we are borne along by it, influenced precisely as we are, to do just the things that we do, the bass lisper said.

And then are cruelly punished for it, said the woman.

Our regiment was being badly cut up by the Baluches, the Brit said. But then the tide turned, and a mess of them surrendered to us, with a white flag, and, well—down into the ditch they went, and the men fired, upon my command (none of them unhappily, mind you), and we threw in their white flag on top of the savages and covered them up. How could I have done otherwise? With time flowing in only one direction and myself made just as I was? With my short temper and my notions of manhood and honor, my schoolboy history of being beaten to within an inch of my life by three older brothers, that rifle feeling so beautiful in my hands and our enemies appearing so loathsome? How was I (how are any of us) to do other than that which we, at that time, actually do?

And did that argument persuade? the woman said.

You know very well, you tart, that it did not! the Brit said. For here I am.

Here we all are, said the Vermonter.

And ever shall be, said the Brit.

Nothing to be done about it, said the bass lisper.

Nothing ever *to* have been done about it, said the woman.

roger bevins iii

Glancing over, I saw a look pass over the Reverend's face—a flicker of resolve, or defiance.

hans vollman

To be grouped with *these,* accepting one's sins so passively, even proudly, with no trace of repentance?

I could not bear it; must I, even now, be beyond all hope?

(Perhaps, I thought, *this* is faith: to believe our God ever receptive to the smallest good intention.)

the reverend everly thomas

Enough, the Vermonter said.

Down to business, said the woman. We have wasted too much effort on this one already.

The previous one? said the Brit. The girl? Much more amenable.

Wonderful child, said the woman. Completely passive.

Never gave us a bit of trouble, said the Brit.

Had our way with her just as pretty as you please, the bass lisper said.

Then again, she did not have all of this "help," said the Vermonter.

True, the Brit said. No one helped her a single bit.

Young man? the woman said. Is it to be *here*? Or on the roof?

roger bevins iii

The lad was silent.

hans vollman

On the roof, the Reverend said. If you please.

Very well, said the woman.

The carapace fell away at once, and the boy was free.

roger bevins iii

If I might request the honor of carrying him up there? the Reverend said.

Certainly, the woman said.

hans vollman

I reached down, picked the boy up.

Ran.

Out of the crypt and into the night.

Ran-skimmed.

Ran-skimmed like the wind.

Toward the only place that now held the slightest hope of affording him refuge.

the reverend everly thomas

LXXXII.

Joyful, joyful!
An exceedingly bold stroke!

roger bevins iii

Bastard! the woman cried out wearily.

hans vollman

Mr. Vollman and I ran-skimmed out of the white stone home in pursuit of the Reverend.

roger bevins iii

A low wave burst out behind us, a moving knee-high wall comprised of whatever substance the demonic beings happened to be inhabiting in that instant (grass, dirt, headstone, statue, bench)—

hans vollman

Which passed us now—

roger bevins iii

(Like children in the surf, we were lifted, then set down again.)

hans vollman

—and overtook the Reverend.

roger bevins iii

Who, slapped and harangued by the matter-blur that plashed up all about him, broke down the small hill near the gardener's shed.

hans vollman

The chapel now coming into sight, we suddenly understood his intention.

roger bevins iii

The demonic beings split into two divisions, as it were, coming up fast on either side of the Reverend, then performed a crossing maneuver, at knee level, tripping him up.

hans vollman

As he fell, to protect the boy, he instinctively rolled on to his back, so as to absorb the brunt of the impact.

roger bevins iii

And they had him.

hans vollman

Had them.

They sought the boy but, seeking the boy, pinioned the Reverend as well.

roger bevins iii

In their frenzy it appeared they were no longer capable of, or interested in, distinguishing between reverend and lad.

hans vollman

By the time we reached the Reverend and the boy, the two were bundled tightly together within a rapidly solidifying new carapace.

roger bevins iii

The Reverend's terrible cries sounding from within.

hans vollman

They have me! he shouted. They have even me! I must—I must go! Good God! Mustn't I? Or be trapped like this, forever—

Go, yes, by all means, save yourself, dear friend! I shouted. Go!

But I don't want to! he shouted. I am afraid!

The choked, garbled quality of his voice told us that the carapace had reached his mouth, and then it seemed it had penetrated even into his brain, and was making him delirious.

That palace, he shouted at the very end. That dreadful diamond palace!

roger bevins iii

Then, from inside the carapace, came the familiar, yet always bone-chilling, firesound associated with the matterlightblooming phenomenon.

hans vollman

And the Reverend was gone.

roger bevins iii

The Reverend's departure creating a temporary vacuity within the carapace—

hans vollman

Mr. Vollman gave the thing a tremendous kick, and caved it in.

roger bevins iii

As we fell enraged upon it, digging and clawing, I could feel the demonic beings within looking askance at us, repulsed by our ferocity, our revived human proclivity for hatred-inspired action. Mr. Bevins drove one arm in up to the elbow. From the other side, I was able to puncture the carapace with a long bough, and situating myself beneath that bough drove up with my knees, and the carapace split open, and Mr. Bevins was able to get his two arms fully inside. Letting out a shout of exertion, he began to pull, and soon, like a foal newly born (as wet, as untidy), the lad tumbled out, and for a second we were able to clearly observe, inside the ruptured carapace, the imprint of the Reverend's face, which had not, I am happy to say, in those final instants, reverted back to the face we had so long associated with him (badly frightened, eyebrows high, the mouth a perfect O of terror), but, rather, his countenance now conveyed a sense of tentative hopefulness—as if he were going into that unknown place content that he had, at any rate, while in this place, done all that he could.

hans vollman

Mr. Vollman snatched up the boy and dashed away.

The demonic beings, flowing out of the remains of the carapace into the earth, gave chase.

Soon, from below, Mr. Vollman's ankles were cuffed, and he tumbled to his knees, and the demonic beings, forming again into tendrils, shot rapidly up his legs and torso and began pioneering out on to his arms.

I raced over, plucked the boy away, dashed off.

And within seconds was myself overrun.

roger bevins iii

I leapt to my feet, raced over, plucked the lad away from Mr. Bevins, dashed off toward the chapel, and, just before I was again overrun, managed to fall forward, through the northernmost side-wall.

I know this place, the lad mumbled.

I expect you do, I said. We all know it.

For many of us, the chapel had served as our portal; our place of disembarkation; the last place we had ever been taken seriously.

hans vollman

The earth around the chapel began to roil.

Even here? I said. Outside this most holy place?

Holy, unholy, all the same to us, said the Brit.

Have a job to do, said the Vermonter.

Are compelled, said the woman.
Go in, send him out, said the Brit.
You merely delay, said the Vermonter.
We are gathering our strength, said the Brit.
Shall be in shortly, said the woman.
With a vengeance, said the Vermonter.
Send him out, snapped the lisper.

roger bevins iii

Mr. Bevins had just stepped in through the wall when, from the darkness at the front of the chapel, a pronounced manly throat-clearing told us we were not alone.

Mr. Lincoln sat in the front row of chairs, where he must have sat during the previous day's service.

hans vollman

LXXXIII.

Tom as we neared front gate Pres catching sight of chapel said he thought he might go over and sit in that quiet place a bit if I did not mind and confided in me that he felt his boy was still here with him and could not shake that feeling but perhaps a few minutes sitting silent in that place of prayer might do the trick.

Declined my offer of lantern saying he would not need it for he saw pretty good in the dark and always had and went off through that very space only yesterday filled with the many hundreds standing on the lawn in the drizzle in their black coats and upraised umbrellas and the sounds of the sad organ from within and I returned to guardhouse which is where I am now writing this while outside his poor little horse's eager hoofs sound against the cobblestone as if his master's proximity causing him to do a stationary horse dance preparatory to long ride home.

Pres in chapel yet.

Manders, op. cit.

LXXXIV.

The stained-glass windows responded dully but substantially to the dim moonlight shining through them.

hans vollman

Suffusing all with a bluish tint.

roger bevins iii

All but the first few rows of chairs had been removed since the previous day's service, and these were somewhat disordered.

hans vollman

Mr. Lincoln sat facing forward, legs thrown out before him, hands clasped in his lap, head lowered.

For a moment I thought he might be sleeping.

But then, as if intuiting our entry, he roused himself and looked around.

roger bevins iii

Curious individuals from across the premises were pouring in through the chapel walls like water through a bad mud dam.

Go in, I said to the lad.

hans vollman

The boy blinked twice.

Went in.

roger bevins iii

By making to sit in his father's lap.

hans vollman

As he must often have done in that previous place.

roger bevins iii

Seated one inside the other now, they occupied the same physical space, the child a contained version of the man.

hans vollman

LXXXV.

(Father Here I am

What should I

If you tell me to go I will

If you tell me stay I will

I wait upon your advice Sir)

I listened for Father's reply

The moonlight swelled All became more blue ish Father's mind was blank blankblankblank

And then

I cannot believe all of this has actually

He began remembering Reviewing Certain things About me

Concerning my illness

What was the name of that woman whose daughter was struck by lightning. In Ponce's hayfield. Just before, walking through, the two of them had been talking about peaches. The different varieties of peaches. Which kind each preferred. For nights after, they found her wandering Ponce's, mumbling about peaches, searching for that juncture of the conversation at which she might jump the breach of time and go back, push the girl aside, take the fatal bolt herself. She could not accept that it had happened, but must go over it and over it.

Now I understand.

That afternoon he brought in five rocks on a tray. Meant to try to find the scientific name of each. The rocks are on that tray yet. In the hallway windowsill near his room. (I believe I shall never be able to move them.)

Toward dusk I found him sitting on the stairs, tray on his knees.
Well, I don't feel so good today, he said.
I put my hand on his head.
Burning.

willie lincoln

LXXXVI.

The fever, which had been diagnosed as a cold, developed into typhoid.

Leech, op. cit.

Typhoid works slowly and cruelly over a period of weeks, depriving the victim of digestive function, perforating the bowels, causing hemorrhaging and peritonitis.

Epstein, op. cit.

The debilitating symptoms of his illness took their toll—high fever, diarrhea, painful cramps, internal hemorrhage, vomiting, profound exhaustion, delirium.

Goodwin, op. cit.

Paregoric may ease the racking abdominal pain; delirium may take the child into a haven of sweet dreams, or it may deliver him into a labyrinth of nightmares.

Epstein, op. cit.

The patient was wandering of mind and did not recognize the distracted loving face of the tall man who bent over him.

Kunhardt and Kunhardt, op. cit.

The President would come in from his work for the country and pace about the room, head in his hands at the agonized moans his poor boy was making.

Flagg, op. cit.

"Kind little words, which are of the same blood as great and holy deeds," flowed from his lips constantly.

In "Lincoln as I Knew Him,"
by Harold Holzer, account of
Elizabeth Todd Grimsley.

Lincoln had the tenderest heart for any one in distress, whether man, beast, or bird.

Holzer, ibid., account of Joshua Fry Speed.

He had a great kindness of heart. His mind was full of tender sensibilities; he was extremely humane.

Wilson and Davis, op. cit., account
of Leonard Swett.

I never in my life associated with a man who seemed so ready to serve another.

Holzer, op. cit., account of John H. Littlefield.

He was certainly a very poor hater.

In "Abraham Lincoln: The True Story
of a Great Life," by William H. Herndon
and Jesse W. Weik.

How that beloved boy's sufferings must have tormented one so naturally sympathetic.

Flagg, op. cit.

Willie Lincoln thrashed and moaned and nothing at all could be done.

Hilyard, op. cit., account of
D. Strumphort, butler.

The burning cheeks, the frantically roving eyes, the low moans of despair, seemed to signal a great torment within and a corresponding desire to escape it, and be himself again, a happy little fellow.

Hohner, op. cit.

In his thrashing young Willie kicked off the gold and purple bedspread. It lay in a heap on the floor.

Sternlet, op. cit.

The yellow trimmings, gold tassels and fringes did not relieve the gloominess of the regal décor, but instead reminded visitors that darkness and death came even to princes.

Epstein, op. cit.

Now the eyes went dim, all that restless motion came to a halt. That stillness seemed the most terrifying thing of all. He was on his own now. None could help or hinder him on the profound journey which, it seemed, had now begun.

Hohner, op. cit.

The death-dew gathered on his brow.

Keckley, op. cit.

In the room of Death, just before the cessation of breath, time seems to stop entirely.

Sternlet, op. cit.

The President could only stand and watch, eyes wide, having no power at all in this new-arrived and brutal realm.

Hohner, op. cit.

LXXXVII.

Wait, the lad said.

He sat there, within his father, a look of consternation on his little face, seeming more upset than comforted by whatever he was hearing.

Come out, I ordered.

I don't understand, he said.

Come out at once, I said.

hans vollman

LXXXVIII.

The body was embalmed on February 22 by Doctors Brown and Alexander, who were assisted by Dr. Wood.

In "Lincoln Lore: Bulletin of the Lincoln Life Foundation," No. 1511, January 1964.

Neither Brown nor Alexander personally embalmed Willie; that job fell to their master embalmer, Henry P. Cattell.

In "Stealing Lincoln's Body," by Thomas J. Craughwell.

Frank T. Sands was the chief undertaker. Perhaps it was he who suggested the precaution of covering the breast of the corpse with the green and white blossoms of the mignonette (*Reseda odorata*), known for its overpoweringly sweet fragrance.

Epstein, op. cit.

The method of Sagnet of Paris was used.

"Lincoln Lore," op. cit.

Sagnet had pioneered the innovative use of zinc chloride.

In "Pausing Death: Nineteenth Century Embalming and the Cult of Immortality," by Steven Wedge and Emily Wedge.

Five quarts of a 20 percent solution of zinc chloride injected through the popliteal artery not only preserved a body for a minimum of two years, but also wrought a wondrous transformation, giving the body the appearance of luminous white marble.

Craughwell, op. cit.

Extravagant claims were made of the Sagnet process, stating that the remains became a "shell in effigy; a sculpture."

"Lincoln Lore," op. cit.

A trestle table was assembled in place for the procedure. The carpets in the Green Room were rolled back and the flooring protected by use of a large square of tenting fabric.

In "The Doctor's Assistant: Memoirs of D. Root," by Donovan G. Root, M.D.

The procedure did not require draining the body of the blood. The boy was undressed and an incision made in the left thigh. The zinc chloride was pumped in using a small-diameter metal pump. No unusual difficulties were encountered. The entry point required a small suture and the boy was re-dressed.

Wedge and Wedge, op. cit.

The mother being distraught, the burial clothes had been selected by the father and sent down to us in an oversized hat-box.

Root, op. cit.

Willie was attired in the usual type of clothing worn for everyday. It consisted of pants, jacket, white stockings, and low-cut shoes. The white shirt collar was turned down over the jacket, and the cuffs were turned back over the sleeves.

In "Abraham Lincoln: From Skeptic to Prophet," by Wayne C. Temple, quoting "Illinois State Journal," July 7, 1871.

We had all of us of the household many times seen that little gray suit on the living boy.

Hilyard, op. cit., account of
D. Strumphort, butler.

Little Willie, pathetically wasted, was dressed in one of his old brown suits, white socks, and low-cut shoes, like an ill-used marionette.

Epstein, op. cit.

He lay with eyes closed—his brown hair parted as we had known it—pale in the slumber of death; but otherwise unchanged, for he was dressed as if for the evening, and held in one of his hands, crossed upon his breast, a bunch of exquisite flowers.

Willis, op. cit.

The President came in for a look—only too early. The trestle table was still up. Jenkins was just gathering up the tarp. The tools of our craft were yet visible in the open box. The pump still gurgled. I was sorry for this. It impeded upon the desired effect. The President blanched noticeably, thanked us, quickly left the room.

Root, op. cit.

LXXXIX.

The boy sat stock-still, eyes very wide indeed.

roger bevins iii

XC.

They buried Willie Lincoln on a day of great wind, that tore the roofs off houses and slashed the flags to ribbons.

Leech, op. cit.

In the procession to Oak Hill Cemetery in Georgetown two white horses drew the hearse bearing the little boy who had known only happiness. But black horses drew the carriage in which sat the worn and grief-stricken President.

Randall, op. cit.

The gale blew the roofs off tall houses, shattered glass windows, leveled fields of military tents, turned muddy streets into canals and canals into rapids. Gusts of wind destroyed several churches and many shacks, uprooted trees, blew out the skylights of the Library of Congress; waves inundated the Long Bridge over the Potomac to Alexandria.

Epstein, op. cit.

The father drove, unseeing, through the wreckage.

Leech, op. cit.

The carriages of the funeral procession stretched for so many blocks that they took a long time to wind their way up to the heights of Georgetown and to the beautiful Oak Hill Cemetery with its crown of oak trees.

Kunhardt and Kunhardt, op. cit.

When the head of the cortege reached Oak Hill Cemetery by way of Washington Street it was found necessary, because of the length of the line to route a part of the line along Bridge Street into High Street. Climbing the hill past the new High Level Reservoir, it turned into Road Street, and proceeded eastward to the cemetery, where the body of William Wallace Lincoln was to be placed in the vault of W. T. Carroll, on Lot 292.

In "Essay on the Death of Willie Lincoln,"
by Mathilde Williams, curator,
Peabody Library Association.

Now all was still and the hundreds of people climbed out of their carriages and walked through the gates of the cemetery to the beautiful little red stone Gothic chapel with its blue-stained windows.

Kunhardt and Kunhardt, op. cit.

At one moment the sun came out and, pouring in through the small windows, painted everything inside with a blue glow, as if at the bottom of the sea, causing a small pause in the prayers, and a feeling of awe among the congregants.

Smith-Hill, op. cit.

Here, over the coffin, more prayers were said by Dr. Gurley.

Kunhardt and Kunhardt, op. cit.

We may be sure,—therefore, bereaved parents, and all the children of sorrow may be sure,—that their affliction has not come forth of the dust, nor has their trouble sprung out of the ground.

It is the well-ordered procedure of their Father and their God. A mysterious dealing they may consider it, but it is still His dealing; and while they mourn He is saying to them, as the Lord Jesus once said to his Disciples when they were perplexed by his conduct, "What I do ye know not now, but ye shall know hereafter."

Gurley, op. cit.

And there sat the man, with a burden on his brain at which the world marvels—bent now with the load at both heart and brain—staggering under a blow like the taking from him of his child!

Willis, op. cit.

The President rose, approached the coffin, stood there alone.

In "The Dark Days," by Francine Cane.

The tension and grief in the chapel were palpable. The President's head, as he spent these last precious moments with his boy, was bent—in prayer, weeping, or consternation, we could not tell.

Smith-Hill, op. cit.

In the distance, shouting. A workman perhaps, directing an effort to clean up after the cataclysmic storm.

Cane, op. cit.

The President turned away from the coffin, it appeared by sheer act of will, and it occurred to me how hard it must be for the man to leave his child behind in a place of such gloom and loneliness, which never, when responsible for the living child, he would have done.

In private correspondence of Mr. Samuel Pierce, by permission of his estate.

He seemed to have aged greatly in the last few days. Many sympathetic eyes & prayers being directed at him, he appeared, then, to come to himself, and left the chapel, a most distressed look upon his face, but not yet giving way to tears.

Smith-Hill, op. cit.

I went up to the President and, taking him by the hand, offered my sincerest condolences.

He did not seem to be listening.
His face lit up with dark wonder.
Willie is dead, he said, as if it had only just then occurred to him.

Pierce, op. cit.

XCI.

The lad stood.

hans vollman

Emerging, in this way, from Mr. Lincoln.

roger bevins iii

Turned to us.

hans vollman

Stricken look on his pale round face.

roger bevins iii

May I tell you something? he said.

How I loved him in that moment. Such an odd little fellow: his long swoop of forelock, roundish protruding belly, rather adult manner.

You are not sick, he said.

hans vollman

Suddenly all was nervousness and agitation.

roger bevins iii

That thing in my box? he said. Has nothing to do with me.

hans vollman

Individuals began edging toward the door.

roger bevins iii

I mean, it does, he said. Or *did*. But now I am—I am something quite apart. From it. I cannot explain.

hans vollman

Stop talking, Mr. Vollman said. You will kindly stop talking at once.

There is a name for what ails us, the boy said. Do you not know it? Do you really not know it?

roger bevins iii

Many were now attempting to flee, causing a bit of a jam at the door.

hans vollman

It is quite amazing, the boy said.

Stop, Mr. Vollman said. Please stop. For the good of all.

Dead, the boy said. Everyone, we are dead!

roger bevins iii

Suddenly, from behind us, there occurred, like lightning-cracks, three rapid-fire repetitions of the familiar, yet always bone-chilling, fire-sound associated with the matterlightblooming phenomenon.

hans vollman

I did not dare to look around to see who had gone.

roger bevins iii

Dead! the lad shouted, almost joyfully, strutting into the middle of the room. Dead, dead, dead!

That word.

That terrible word.

hans vollman

Purdy, Bark, and Ella Blow were flailing within a window casement, like trapped birds, weakened and compromised by the lad's reckless pronouncements.

roger bevins iii

Verna Blow stood below, pleading with her mother to come down.

hans vollman

Now look, Mr. Vollman said to the boy. You are wrong. If what you say is true—who is it that is saying it?

Who is *hearing* it? I said.

Who is speaking to you now? said Mr. Vollman.

To whom do we speak? I said.

roger bevins iii

But he would not be silenced.

hans vollman

Tore away years of work and toil with each thoughtless phrase.

roger bevins iii

Father said it, he said. Said I am dead. Why would he say that, if it weren't true? I just now heard him say it. I heard him, that is, remembering having said it.

We had no answer for this.

hans vollman

It did not, indeed, seem to us (knowing him as we now knew him) that Mr. Lincoln would lie about such a momentous thing.

I have to say, it gave me pause.

In my early days here, I only now recalled, I had, yes, for a brief period, understood myself to be—

roger bevins iii

But then you saw the truth. Saw that you moved around, and spoke, and thought, and that, therefore, must be merely *sick*, with some previously unknown malady, and could not possibly be—

hans vollman

It gave me pause.

roger bevins iii

I was good, the lad said. Or tried to be. I want to do good now. And go where I should. Where I should have gone in the first place. Father will not return here. And none of us will ever be allowed back to that previous place.

hans vollman

He was hopping with joy now, like a toddler too full of water.

Look, join me, he said. Everyone! Why stay? There's nothing to it. We're done. Don't you see?

roger bevins iii

Purdy, Bark, and Ella Blow, within the window casement, went, in a triply blinding blast of the matterlightblooming phenomenon.

hans vollman

Followed quickly by Verna Blow, there below, unwilling to endure (as she had been made to endure, for so long, in that previous place) an existence without her mother.

roger bevins iii

I knew it! the lad shouted. I knew something was off with me!

hans vollman

His flesh seemed thin as parchment; tremors ran through his body.

roger bevins iii

His form (as sometimes happens to those about to go) began flickering between the various selves he had been in that previous place: purple newborn, squalling naked infant, jelly-faced toddler, feverish boy on sick-bed.

hans vollman

Then, with no change in size at all (i.e., while still child-sized), he displayed his various *future*-forms (forms he had, alas, never succeeded in attaining):

Nervous young man in wedding-coat;

Naked husband, wet-groined with recent pleasure;

Young father leaping out of bed to light a candle at a child's cry;

Grieving widower, hair gone white;

Bent ancient fellow with an ear trumpet, athwart a stump, swatting at flies.

roger bevins iii

All the while seeming quite innocent of these alterations.

hans vollman

Oh, it was nice, he said sadly. So nice there. But we can't go back. To how we were. All we can do is what we *should*.

roger bevins iii

Then, drawing a deep breath, closing his eyes—

hans vollman

He went.

roger bevins iii

The lad went.

hans vollman

Never before had Mr. Vollman or I been so proximate to the matter-lightblooming phenomenon and its familiar, but always bone-chilling, firesound.

roger bevins iii

The resulting explosion knocked us off our feet.

hans vollman

Squinting up from the floor, we caught a brief last glimpse of the pale baby-face, a pair of anticipation-fisted hands, an arched little back.

roger bevins iii

And he was gone.

hans vollman

His little gray suit lingering behind for the briefest instant.

roger bevins iii

XCII.

I am Willie I am Willie I am even yet

Am not

Willie

Not willie but somehow

Less

More

All is Allowed now All is allowed me now All is allowed light-lightlight me now

Getting up out of bed and going down to the party, allowed

Candy bees, allowed

Chunks of cake, allowed!

Punch (even rum punch), allowed!

Let that band play louder!

Swinging from the chandelier, allowed; floating up to ceiling, allowed; going to window to have a look out, allowed allowed allowed!

Flying out window, allowed, allowed (the entire laughing party of guests happily joining behind me, urging me to please, yes, fly away) (saying oh, he feels much better now, he does not seem sick at all!)!

Whatever that former fellow (willie) had, must now be given back (is given back gladly) as it never was mine (never his) and therefore is not being taken away, not at all!

As I (who was of willie but is no longer (merely) of willie) return

To such beauty.

willie lincoln

XCIII.

There in his seat, Mr. Lincoln startled.

roger bevins iii

Like a schoolboy jolting suddenly awake in class.

hans vollman

Looked around.

roger bevins iii

Momentarily unsure, it seemed, of where he was.

hans vollman

Then got to his feet and made for the door.

roger bevins iii

The lad's departure having set him free.

hans vollman

So quickly did he move that he passed through us before we could step aside.

roger bevins iii

And again, briefly, we knew him.

hans vollman

XCIV.

His boy was gone; his boy was no more.

hans vollman

His boy was nowhere; his boy was everywhere.

roger bevins iii

There was nothing here for him now.

hans vollman

His boy was no more *here* than *anyplace else,* that is. There was nothing special, anymore, about *this* place.

roger bevins iii

His continued presence here was wrong; was wallowing.

hans vollman

His having come here at all a detour and a weakness.

roger bevins iii

His mind was freshly inclined toward *sorrow;* toward the fact that the world was full of sorrow; that everyone labored under some burden of sorrow; that all were suffering; that whatever way one took in this world, one must try to remember that all were suffering (none content; all wronged, neglected, overlooked, misunderstood), and therefore one must do what one could to lighten the load of those with whom one came into contact; that his current state of sorrow was not uniquely his, not at all, but, rather, its like had been felt, would yet be felt, by scores of others, in all times, in every time, and must not be prolonged or exaggerated, because, in this state, he could be of no help to anyone and, given that his position in the world situated him to be either of great help or great harm, it would not do to stay low, if he could help it.

hans vollman

All were in sorrow, or had been, or soon would be.

roger bevins iii

It was the nature of things.

hans vollman

Though on the surface it seemed every person was different, this was not true.

roger bevins iii

At the core of each lay suffering; our eventual end, the many losses we must experience on the way to that end.

hans vollman

We must try to see one another in this way.

roger bevins iii

As suffering, limited beings—

hans vollman

Perennially outmatched by circumstance, inadequately endowed with compensatory graces.

roger bevins iii

His sympathy extended to all in this instant, blundering, in its strict logic, across all divides.

hans vollman

He was leaving here broken, awed, humbled, diminished.

roger bevins iii

Ready to believe anything of this world.

hans vollman

Made less rigidly himself through this loss.

roger bevins iii

Therefore quite powerful.

hans vollman

Reduced, ruined, remade.

roger bevins iii

Merciful, patient, dazzled.

hans vollman

And yet.

roger bevins iii

And yet.

He was in a fight. Although those he fought were also suffering, limited beings, he must—

hans vollman

Obliterate them.

roger bevins iii

Kill them and deny them their livelihood and force them back into the fold.

hans vollman

He must (*we* must, we felt) do all *we* could, in light of the many soldiers lying dead and wounded, in open fields, all across the land, weeds violating their torsos, eyeballs pecked out or dissolving, lips hideously retracted, rain-soaked/blood-soaked/snow-crusted letters scattered about them, to ensure that we did not, as we trod that difficult path we were now well upon, blunder, blunder further (we had blundered so badly already) and, in so blundering, ruin more, more of these boys, each of whom was once dear to someone.

Ruinmore, ruinmore, we felt, *must endeavor not to ruinmore.*

Our grief must be defeated; it must not become our master, and make us ineffective, and put us even deeper into the ditch.

roger bevins iii

We must, to do the maximum good, bring the thing to its swiftest halt and—

hans vollman

Kill.

roger bevins iii

Kill more efficiently.

hans vollman

Hold nothing back.

roger bevins iii

Make the blood flow.

hans vollman

Bleed and bleed the enemy until his good sense be reborn.

roger bevins iii

The swiftest halt to the thing (therefore the greatest mercy) might be the bloodiest.

hans vollman

Must end suffering by causing more suffering.

roger bevins iii

We were low, lost, an object of ridicule, had almost nothing left, were failing, must take some action to halt our fall, and restore ourselves *to* ourselves.

hans vollman

Must win. Must win the thing.

roger bevins iii

His heart dropped at the thought of the killing.

hans vollman

Did the thing merit it. Merit the killing. On the surface it was a technicality (mere Union) but seen deeper, it was something more. How should men live? How could men live? Now he recalled the boy he had been (hiding from Father to read Bunyan; raising rabbits to gain a few coins; standing in town as the gaunt daily parade drawled out the hard talk hunger made; having to reel back when one of those more fortunate passed merrily by in a carriage), feeling strange and odd (smart too, superior), long-legged, always knocking things over, called names (Ape Lincoln, Spider, Ape-a-ham, Monstrous-Tall), but also thinking, quietly, there inside himself, that he might someday get something for himself. And then, going out to get it, he had found the way clear—his wit was quick, people liked him for his bumbling and his ferocity of purpose, and the peach orchards and haystacks and young girls and ancient wild meadows drove him nearly mad with their beauty, and strange animals moved in lazy mobs along muddy rivers, rivers crossable only with the aid of some old rowing hermit who spoke a language barely English, and all of it, all of that bounty, was *for everyone,* for everyone to use, seemingly put here to teach a man to be free, to teach that a man *could* be free, that any man, any free white man, could come from as low a place as *he* had (a rutting sound coming from the Cane cabin, he had looked in through the open door and seen two pairs of still-socked feet and a baby toddling past, steadying herself by grasping one of the rutters' feet), and even a young fellow who had seen *that,* and lived among *those,* might rise, here, as high as he was inclined to go.

And that, against this: the king-types who would snatch the apple from your hand and claim to have grown it, even though what they had, had come to them intact, or been gained unfairly (the nature of that unfairness perhaps being just that they had been born stronger, more clever, more energetic than others), and who, having seized the apple, would eat it so proudly, they seemed to think that not only had they grown it, but had invented the very idea of fruit, too, and the cost of this lie fell on the hearts of the low (Mr. Bellway rushing his children off their Sangamon porch as he and Father slumped past with that heavy bag of grain drooping between them).

Across the sea fat kings watched and were gleeful, that something begun so well had now gone off the rails (as down South similar kings watched), and if it went off the rails, so went the whole kit, forever, and if someone ever thought to start it up again, well, it would be said (and said truly): The rabble cannot manage itself.

Well, the rabble could. The rabble would.

He would lead the rabble in managing.

The thing would be won.

roger bevins iii

Our Willie would not wish us hobbled in that attempt by a vain and useless grief.

hans vollman

In *our* mind the lad stood atop a hill, merrily waving to us, urging us to be brave and resolve the thing.

roger bevins iii

But (*we* stopped ourselves short) was this not just wishful thinking? Weren't we, in order to enable ourselves to go on, positing from our boy a blessing we could not possibly verify?

Yes.

Yes we were.

hans vollman

But we must do so, and believe it, or else we were ruined.

roger bevins iii

And we must not be ruined.

hans vollman

But must go on.

roger bevins iii

We saw all of this in the instant it took Mr. Lincoln to pass through us.

hans vollman

And then he was out the door, and into the night.

roger bevins iii

XCV.

We black folks had not gone into the church with the others.

Our experience having been that white people are not especially fond of having us in their churches. Unless it is to hold a baby, or prop up or hand-fan some old one.

Then here came that tall white man out the door, right at me.

I held my ground as he passed through and got something along the lines of *I will go on, I will. With God's help. Though it seems killing must go hard against the will of God. Where might God stand on this. He has shown us. He could stop it. But has not. We must see God not as a Him (some linear rewarding fellow) but an IT, a great beast beyond our understanding, who wants something from us, and we must give it, and all we may control is the spirit in which we give it and the ultimate end which the giving serves. What end does IT wish served? I do not know. What IT wants, it seems, for now, is blood, more blood, and to alter things from what they are, to what IT wills they should be. But what that new state is, I do not know, and patiently wait to learn, even as those three thousand fallen stare foul-eyed at me, working dead hands anxiously, asking, What end might this thing yet attain, that will make our terrible sacrifice worthwh—*

Then he was through me and I was glad.

Near the front gate stood Mr. Havens, square in that white man's path, as I had been, but doing, then, something I had not the nerve (nor desire) to do.

mrs. francis hodge

XCVI.

I don't know what came over me. Never, in that previous place, had I been a rash person. What need had I to be? Mr. Conner, and his good wife, and all of their children and grandchildren were like *family* to me. Never was I separated from my own wife or children. We ate well, were never beaten. They had given us a small but attractive yellow cottage. It was a happy arrangement, all things considered.

So I don't know what came over me.

As that gentleman passed through, I felt a kinship.

And decided to stay a bit.

Therein.

So there we were, moving along together, me matching him step for step. Which was not easy. His legs were *long*. I extended my legs, to match his, and extended all of myself, and we were the same size, and *out*, upon horseback and (forgive me) the thrill of once again riding a horse was too much, and I—I stayed. Therein. What a thrill it was! To be doing what I wished. Without having been ordered to do so, without having sought anyone's permission. The ceiling of a lifelong house flew off, if I may put it that way. I knew, of the instant, vast tracts of Indiana and Illinois (full towns in their complete layout and the nature of the hospitality of specific houses therein, though I had never been in either of those places), and came to feel that this fellow—well, my goodness, I will not say what office it seemed to me that he held. I began to feel afraid, occupying someone so accomplished. And yet, I was comfortable in there. And suddenly, wanted him to *know* me. My life. To know *us*. Our lot. I don't know why I felt that way but I did. He had no *aversion* to me, is how I might put it. Or rather, he had once had such an aversion, still bore traces of it, but, in examining that aversion, pushing it into the light, had somewhat, already, eroded it. He was an open book. An *opening* book. That had just been opened up somewhat wider. By sorrow. And—by us. By all of us, black and white, who had so recently mass-inhabited him. He had not, it seemed, gone unaffected by that event. Not at all. It had made him sad. Sadder. *We* had. All of us, white and black, had made him sadder, with our sadness. And now, though it sounds strange to say, he was making *me* sadder with *his* sadness, and I thought, Well, sir, if we are going to make a sadness party of it, I have some sadness about which I think someone as powerful as you might like to know. And I thought, then, as hard as I could, of Mrs. Hodge, and Elson, and Litzie, and of all I had heard during our long occupancy in that pit regarding their many troubles and degradations, and called to mind, as well, several others of our race I had known and loved (my Mother; my wife; our children, Paul, Timothy, Gloria; Rance P., his sister Bee; the four little Cushmans), and all the things that *they* had endured, thinking, Sir, if you are as powerful as I feel that you are, and as inclined toward us as you seem to be, endeavor to *do* something for us, so that we might do something for ourselves. We are ready, sir; are angry, are capable, our hopes are coiled up so tight as to be deadly, or holy: turn us loose, sir, let us at it, let us show what we can do.

thomas havens

XCVII.

Elson and Litzie had been by the chapel door, listening in.

Now they trot-skimmed over, holding hands.

That little white boy? Litzie said.

Said we are dead, said Elson.

mrs. francis hodge

Goodness, said Mrs. Hodge.

elson farwell

All these years, in our pit, I had treasured up the notion that someday Annalise and Benjamin, my children, would—

Would what? Join me? Someday join me? Here? It was ludicrous.

Suddenly I saw just how ludicrous.

Poor me.

Poor me, all of those years.

They would never join me here. They would age and die and be laid to rest *there*, in those far-flung locales to which they had been taken (when taken from me). They would not come *here*. And anyway, why would I want that? I had wanted it, somehow, while I only waited, believing myself *paused*. But now, now that I—

Now that I knew I was dead, I wanted for them only to go to where they *should*. Directly there. Wherever that was. And feeling that way, saw that I ought to go there myself.

I looked at Litzie in our old way, as if to say: Lady, what do you think?

I'll do what you do, Mrs. Hodge, Litzie said. You always been like a mother to me.

mrs. francis hodge

Sad though.

I'd only just got my voice back, and now it was time to leave.

litzie wright

Elson? I said.

No, he said. If such things as *goodness* and *brotherhood* and *redemption* exist, and may be attained, these must sometimes require blood, vengeance, the squirming terror of the former perpetrator, the vanquishing of the heartless oppressor. I intend to stay. Here. Until I have had my revenge. Upon someone.

(Such a dear boy. So proud. So dramatic.)

We are dead, I said.

Here I am, he said. I am here.

I said no more—for if he wished to stay, I would not impede him.

We all must do what we like.

Ready? I said to Litzie.

As if for old times' sake, she gave me the double-eyed blink, which had always meant: Yes.

mrs. francis hodge

XCVIII.

Dear Brother, a post-script—After writing the above went to bed—Some time later woke to sound of horse's hooves—I summoned Grace & she helped me into the wheeled chair & to the window—And who should be leaving but Mr. L. himself—I swear it—Looking ever so weary & stooped in the saddle as he rode away—I opened the window & shouted down to "good old Manders" to confirm—It was indeed the Pres—What must be the extent of his heartache for him to have come here at this cold & cruel hr of the night?

Now I must have Grace help me back to bed—Am doing my best to summon her only when necessary, as she has been out of sorts with me lately—Always in a bad temper & never jolly with me anymore—as if sick of me, & who could blame her—it is not happy to be at the beck & call of one so immobilized—& I cannot blame her for I recently am having more pain, & my good spirits often compromised—but she is no friend—Of this I must constantly remind myself—She is hired, by us, to care for me—And that is ALL.

Brother, when do you come home? I know you wander for your own purposes—but find it hard to believe you are not lonely—Or perhaps you have charmed some Prairie lady—Your sister is tired & lonely & sick—Do you not love me, do you not wish to see me again?—Pls come home—I do not wish to alarm you—Do not say these things to force you home but feel so poorly lately. Weak & drifting in mind & unable to eat—Is it not right that we who love one another, should be together?

Please come home. I miss you so. And have no real friend here in this place.

Yr loving sister,

Isabelle.

Perkins, op. cit.

XCIX.

As Pres emerged from chapel I hightailed it out of guardhouse to unlock gate Pres went out saying nothing seeming distracted reached over gave my forearm warm squeeze then hopped upon the back of his little horse and I thought whole caboodle might go over on its side but no that little horsehero steeling himself clopped away quite dignified as if he meant to protect Pres's reputation by acting as if Pres's feet were not nearly scraping the ground and I tell you Tom that noble nag might have been bearing Hercules or G Washington for all the pride in his step as they disappeared down R Street into chilly night.

As I was locking back up Tom had feeling of being watched and looked up and saw that our "mystery girl" from across the street sat her faithful post at her window and lifting said window from her sitting position with considerable effort called across to me was that Pres who just rode off and I called back yes indeed and it was sad Tom as I have known her or seen her at least since she was a little girl who could still walk and run with all the others and now she must be nearly 30 and feeling kindly inclined toward her now I called up that she best shut the window for the cold for I had heard she was not well and she thanked me for my concern and said it was a sad thing wasn't it about Pres's son and I said oh very sad indeed and she said she thought the child must surely be in a better place and I said I hoped so and prayed so and our voices hung there as if we were last living souls on earth and goodnight said I and goodnight said she and brought her window down and soon enough her light went out.

Manders, op. cit.

C.

A mass exodus from the chapel ensued, our cohort fleeing out through all four walls at once.

hans vollman

Many succumbing even while in motion.

roger bevins iii

Mr. Bevins and I rushed out together, as the inky night around the chapel lit up with multiple instances of the matterlightblooming phenomenon.

hans vollman

All was chaos.

roger bevins iii

The pale smock of the beautiful raped mulatto floated down, still stained with bloody handprints at the hips.

hans vollman

Followed by the large unoccupied dress of Mrs. Hodge.

roger bevins iii

The air was filled with curses, shouts, the hissing velocity-sounds of our dear friends desperately rushing away through bushes and low-hanging trees.

hans vollman

Several had been so severely infected with doubt that locomotion now became impossible.

roger bevins iii

These slumped wearily against stones, crawled weakly along pathways, lay draped and broken-seeming across benches, as if dropped from the sky.

hans vollman

Many succumbing from these undignified positions.

roger bevins iii

Now across the chapel lawn charged Lieutenant Stone.

hans vollman

Heading directly for Mr. Farwell.

roger bevins iii

Clear thee away, cease Contaminating this Holy place, SHARD.

As I am the Man among all here who has been in this Place the longest (the number of my Nights here being beyond TWENTY THOUSAND, and the Number of Souls who, coming to this place, have, through Cowardice and Flinching, since departed anon, by my latest count, nearing NINE HUNDRED), who shall Manage things here if not me, and I will be DAMNED and DAMNED GOOD if the current chaos shall be exploited by a SHARD-MAN as an excuse to loaf!

lieutenant cecil stone

Even the Lieutenant's extreme self-confidence seemed affected by the recent confusion, for he did not grow any taller during this diatribe and seemed, even, to shrink a little.

roger bevins iii

The Lieutenant ordered Mr. Farwell back to work, back to whatever work had been assigned him, by whichever white person had assigned it, at which time Mr. Farwell seized the Lieutenant by the collar and threw him roughly down upon his back.

hans vollman

The Lieutenant demanded to know how Mr. Farwell dare touch a white man in anger, and commanded Farwell to let him up; Mr. Farwell refusing, the Lieutenant kicked Farwell in the chest, and Farwell flew back, and the Lieutenant leapt to his feet and, straddling Farwell, began beating him about the head with his fists. In desperation Farwell groped about for a nearby path stone and swung it into the Lieutenant's head, causing the Lieutenant to fall to the ground and his tricorne to fly off. Farwell then positioned one knee upon the Lieutentant's chest and used the stone to smash the Lieutenant's skull into a flat pulpy mass, after which he stumbled away and sat on the ground disconsolately, head in hands, weeping.

roger bevins iii

The Lieutenant's head quickly re-forming, he revived and, catching sight of the weeping Mr. Farwell, barked out that he was not aware a SHARD could weep, since to weep one must possess human emotions, and again ordered Mr. Farwell back to work, back to whatever work had been assigned him, by whichever white person had assigned it, and again Mr. Farwell seized the Lieutenant by the collar, and threw him down upon his back, and again the Lieutenant demanded to know how Mr. Farwell dare touch a white man in anger and commanded Farwell to let him up, and, Mr. Farwell again refusing, the Lieutenant again kicked Farwell in the chest—

hans vollman

And so on.

roger bevins iii

It was still going on as we fled the scene.

hans vollman

Showed no sign of abating.

roger bevins iii

Was proceeding with a fury that suggested the two might well fight on into eternity.

hans vollman

Unless some fundamental and unimaginable alteration of reality should occur.

roger bevins iii

CI.

Mr. Vollman and I ran-skimmed desperately toward our home-places.

roger bevins iii

Shaken.

hans vollman

Even we were shaken.

roger bevins iii

Even Mr. Bevins and I were shaken.

hans vollman

Brother, what are we to do? I called over.

Here we are, Mr. Vollman called back. Look at me. Here I am. Who is it—who is it that speaks? Who is it hears my speaking?

But we were shaken.

roger bevins iii

We came now upon the disreputable Barons, collapsed in a heap atop the Constantine sick-mound (an unremarkable limestone slab, cracked at one corner, marred by bird droppings over many decades—

hans vollman

For someone, long ago, had planted a small tree overhead, to shade Constantine from the sun).

roger bevins iii

Get up, get up.

No f——ing stopping. No f——ing thinking.

eddie baron

I ain't. I ain't f——ing thinking.

I just don't feel good.

betsy baron

Look at me, look at me.

Remember that time we lived in that f——ing beautiful field? With the kids? That, uh, spacious meadow?

In that tent? Remember that? After f——ing Donovan evicted us from that s——hole by the river? Those were the days, hah?

eddie baron

That was no f——ing spacious meadow! You piece of s——! That was where all the f——ing scum of the earth came to s—— and drop their G———ed garbage!

betsy baron

But what a view, eh? Not many kids get that view. We could look out our tent-flap, and right there: the f——ing White House.

eddie baron

But first you had to walk around the G———n trash heap. While watching out for those big f——ing rats. And that gang of Hessian gropers that f——ing lived in there.

betsy baron

They never groped you though.

eddie baron

Bulls——! I had to burn one f——er's leg with a shovelful of hot coals! To get him off me! Came right in the f——ing tent! In front of the f——ing kids! No wonder they never come see us! We been here—how long we been here? A pretty f——ing long time. And they never come once.

betsy baron

F—— them! Right? Those f——ing ingrate snakes have no G———ed right to blame us for a f——ing thing until they walk a f——ing mile in our G———ed shoes and neither f——ing one of the little s——heads ever walked even—

eddie baron

Eddie? No.
They was our kids.
We f——ed it up.

betsy baron

No f——ing sad s——.
And no f——ing stopping. No f——ing thinking.
You know why?
We want to f——ing stay! Got plenty of celebrating left to f——ing do, right?

eddie baron

Eddie.
We're f——ing dead, Eddie.
Love you, you f——ing f——er.

betsy baron

No.
No no no. Don't. Don't do it.
Stay the f—— with me, kid.

eddie baron

Her flesh became thin as parchment. Tremors ran through her body. Her form flickered between the various selves she had been in that previous place (too debauched and impoverished and shameful to mention) and then between the various future-forms she had, alas, never succeeded in attaining: attentive mother; mindful baker of bread and cakes; sober church-attender; respected soft-spoken grandmother surrounded by her adoring, clean brood.

roger bevins iii

Then came the familiar, yet always bone-chilling, firesound associated with the matterlightblooming phenomenon.

hans vollman

And she was gone.

roger bevins iii

Her threadbare and malodorous clothing raining down all around.

hans vollman

Mr. Baron let loose a prodigious howl of obscenities and succumbed, albeit reluctantly, compelled by his inordinate affection for that lady, the color of his matterlightblooming phenomenon not the usual luminous white, but, rather, a dingy gray.

roger bevins iii

Smelling of tobacco, sweat, and whiskey, his clothes came raining down.

hans vollman

And a racing form, and an obscene cartoon.

roger bevins iii

CII.

Suddenly Mr. Bevins did not look well.

His flesh was thin as parchment. Tremors ran through his body.

hans vollman

So many memories were flooding back.

I recalled a certain morning. The morning of my—

The morning that I—

I had seen Gilbert. At the baker's.

Yes. Yes I had.

My God.

He was—ah, most painful! He was *with someone*. A man. Dark-haired, tall. Broad-chested. Gilbert whispered something to him and they shared a laugh. At my expense, it seemed. The world went flat. It seemed a stage-set built for the telling of a specific joke, to be told on me: having been born with my propensity, I would find Gilbert, come to love him, but would not be able to be with him (for he wished to "live correctly"), and then the punch line: me, crestfallen in that baker's doorway, loaf in hand, the two of them approaching, pausing—the whisper, the laugh—and they broke around on either side of me, this new fellow (he was so beautiful) raising an eyebrow, as if to say: *That*? *That* is him?

Then another killing laugh-burst.

I rushed home and—

Proceeded.

roger bevins iii

Mr. Bevins dropped to his knees.

His form flickered between the various selves he had been in that previous place:

An effeminate but affectionate young boy, much fussed over by a family of sisters;

A diligent student, crouched over multiplication tables;

A naked young man in a carriage house, reaching over to tenderly kiss that Gilbert;

A good son, posed between his parents for a daguerreotype on the occasion of his birthday;

A red-faced distraught disaster, tears rolling down his face, butcher knife in hand, porcelain tub in his lap.

Do you remember, he said. When I first came here? You were so kind to me. Calmed me down. Convinced me to stay. Do you remember?

I was happy to be of service, I said.

I just remembered something else, he said, in a tone of wonder. Your wife once came to visit.

hans vollman

I do not recall any such occurrence, Mr. Vollman replied stiffly. My wife, believing my recovery best aided by a period of solitude, prefers not to visit.

Friend, I said. Enough. Let us speak honestly. I am remembering many things. And I suspect that you are, too.

Not at all, Mr. Vollman said.

A plump, beaming woman came here, I said. A year or so ago. And recounted many things, happy things concerning her life (her numerous children, her excellent husband), and thanked you—thanked *you*, imagine—for your early kindness to her, which had, as she put it, "allowed me to deliver myself, unsullied, to he who would prove to be the great love of my life." She thanked you for placing her "on the path to love," and for never (never once) being unkind to her, but always gentle, and dear, and considerate. "A true friend," she called you.

Tears were rolling down Mr. Vollman's face.

She did you the honor, sir, of coming to say goodbye and, standing at your grave, explained that she would not, in future, be able to join you *there*, as she must, instead, eventually, lie beside this new fellow, her husband, who was—

Please, Mr. Vollman said.

Who was much younger, I said. Than you. Closer, that is, to her own age.

You, Mr. Vollman said abruptly. You cut your wrists and bled to death on your kitchen floor.

Yes, I said. Yes I did.

Many years ago, he said.

So many years ago, I said.

Ah, God, Mr. Vollman said, and his flesh grew thin as parchment, and tremors ran through his body, and his form began to flicker between the various selves he had been in that previous place:

Fresh-faced apprentice in an ink-stained smock;

Young widower, wiping away tears for his first wife, fingernails blue-rimmed with his work, despite an obsessive pre-funeral scrubbing;

Lonely middle-aged fellow, with no hopes at all, who only worked and drank and (in a depressed state) occasionally whored;

A heavy-set, limping, wooden-toothed forty-six-year-old printer, glimpsing, from across the parlor, at the Wicketts', upon New Year's Day, a radiant young woman in a lime dress (little more than a girl, really), and in that moment, he felt himself no longer old, but young (interesting, vital, dashing), and, for the first time in years, felt he had something to offer, and someone to whom he hoped he might be allowed to offer it.

roger bevins iii

Shall we? Mr. Bevins said. Shall we go together?

And assumed his various future-forms (forms he had never, alas, succeeded in attaining):

A fine-looking young man on the prow of a ship, gazing off at a row of yellow and blue houses just coming into view upon a distant shoreline (and on that voyage he had been fucked and fucked well by a Brazilian engineer, who had taught him much and given him much pleasure) (and now Mr. Bevins knew that *that* life was for him, whether it be good or not in God's eyes);

The contented lover, for many years now, of a gentle, bearded pharmacist named Reardon;

A prosperous, chubby, middle-aged fellow, nursing poor Reardon through his final illness;

An old geezer of nearly a hundred, blessedly free of all desire (for man, food, breath) being driven to church in some sort of miracle vehicle, before which stood no horse, and which went about on rubber wheels, loud as some perpetually firing cannon.

hans vollman

Yes, all right, Mr. Vollman said. Let us go. Together.

roger bevins iii

And it seemed we had passed the point of choosing. The knowledge of what we were was strong within us now, and would not be denied.

hans vollman

And yet something held us back.

roger bevins iii

We knew what.

hans vollman

Who.

roger bevins iii

Of one mind now, we flew-skimmed east (erratically, caroming off boulders and hillocks and the walls of stone homes, like wounded birds, feeling nothing but urgency to reach our destination), flickering on and off, weak and growing weaker, sustained, barely, by some lingering, dissipating belief in our own reality, east and east and east, until we reached the edge of that uninhabited wilderness of some several hundred yards.

hans vollman

That ended in the dreaded iron fence.

roger bevins iii

CIII.

The Traynor girl lay as usual, trapped against and part of the fence, manifesting at that moment as a scaled-down smoking wreck of a rail car, several dozen charred and expiring individuals trapped within her barking out the most obscene demands as Miss Traynor's "wheels" turned mercilessly upon several hogs, who (we were given to understand) had caused the crash, and possessed human faces and voices, and were crying out most piteously as the wheels turned and turned and crushed and re-crushed them, giving off the smell of burning pork.

hans vollman

We had come to apologize.

roger bevins iii

For our cowardice at the time of her initial doom.

hans vollman

Which had always, in every minute since, gnawed at us.

roger bevins iii

Our first huge failing.

hans vollman

Our initial abandonment of the better nature we had brought with us from that previous place.

roger bevins iii

Standing outside the burning car, I called in.

Can you hear me, dear? I shouted. There is something we wish to say.

hans vollman

The train shifted a bit on its tracks, and flames leapt up, and several of the hogs who had caused the crash turned to us and, in a beautiful American dialect that came out of their perfectly formed human faces, told us, in no uncertain terms, that she could not and would not be saved, and hated it all, and hated us all, and if we did, indeed, care for her, why not leave her alone, for our presence aggravated her already considerable torment, reminding her, as it did, of the hopes she had held in that previous place, and of who she had been upon first arriving here.

roger bevins iii

A spinning young girl.

hans vollman

In a summer frock of continually shifting color.

roger bevins iii

We are sorry, I shouted in. Sorry that we did not do more to convince you to go, back when you still had the chance.

We were afraid, Mr. Bevins said. Afraid for ourselves.

Anxious, I said. Anxious that we might fail in our endeavor.

We felt we must conserve our resources, Mr. Bevins said.

We are sorry this happened to you, I said.

You did not deserve it, Mr. Bevins said.

And sorry, especially, that we did not stay to console you, as you went down, I said.

You did rather slink away, said one of the hogs.

hans vollman

Mr. Vollman's face contorted with the memory.

Then something changed, and he looked strong and vital, like the man he must have been in his shop, a man who would not have slunk away from much of anything at all.

And sped through his various future-forms:

A beaming fellow in a disordered bed, the morning after he and Anna would have consummated their marriage (she gleefully threw her head upon his chest, and reached between his legs, eager to begin again);

A father of twin girls, who looked like paler, smaller Annas;

A retired printer with bad knees, helped along a boardwalk by that same Anna, older now herself but still beautiful, and as they went along, they spoke confidentially back and forth, somewhat habitually, not always agreeing, in a code that seemed to have developed between them, about the twins, now mothers themselves.

Mr. Vollman turned to me, smiling in a pained but kindly way.

None of that ever was, he said. And it never will be.

Then he drew a deep breath.

And stepped into the burning train.

roger bevins iii

I could see Miss Traynor there, in what had been the dining car, her face clearly visible within the striped lavender wallpaper.

hans vollman

Younge Mr Bristol desired me, younge Mr Fellowes and Mr Delway desired me, of an evening they would sit on the grass around me and in their eyes burned the fiercest kindest Desire.

It was all very

Then Mother would send Annie to come and

I want ed so much to hold a dear Babe.

You might sir

You might sire do me a service A great service

I know very wel I do not look as prety as I onseh.

You might try
Might at least try
Do it here. Do it now Wont you
Blow this fuk cok ass ravage train up. Sir.
With yr going
If you pls It mite free me Dont know Cant say for sure
But have been so unhappy here so long.

elise traynor

I will try, I said.

hans vollman

From within the train came the familiar yet always bone-chilling fire-sound of the matterlightblooming phenomenon.

The train began to vibrate, the hogs to squeal.

I threw myself down on the good and blessed earth, soon to be mine no more.

The train exploded. Seats rained down, hog-parts rained down, menus rained down, luggage, newspapers, umbrellas, ladies' hats, men's shoes, cheap novels rained down.

Rising to my knees I saw that, where the train had been, was now only the dreaded iron fence.

And there was nothing left for me to do, but go.

Though the things of the world were strong with me still.

Such as, for example: a gaggle of children trudging through a side-blown December flurry; a friendly match-share beneath some collision-tilted streetlight; a frozen clock, bird-visited within its high tower; cold water from a tin jug; toweling off one's clinging shirt post–June rain.

Pearls, rags, buttons, rug-tuft, beer-froth.

Someone's kind wishes for you; someone remembering to write; someone noticing that you are not at all at ease.

A bloody roast death-red on a platter; a hedgetop under-hand as you flee late to some chalk-and-woodfire-smelling schoolhouse.

Geese above, clover below, the sound of one's own breath when winded.

The way a moistness in the eye will blur a field of stars; the sore place on the shoulder a resting toboggan makes; writing one's beloved's name upon a frosted window with a gloved finger.

Tying a shoe; tying a knot on a package; a mouth on yours; a hand on yours; the ending of the day; the beginning of the day; the feeling that there will always be a day ahead.

Goodbye, I must now say goodbye to all of it.

Loon-call in the dark; calf-cramp in the spring; neck-rub in the parlor; milk-sip at end of day.

Some bandy-legged dog proudly back-ploughs the grass to cover its modest shit; a cloud-mass down-valley breaks apart over the course of a brandy-deepened hour; louvered blinds yield dusty beneath your dragging finger, and it is nearly noon and you must decide; you have seen what you have seen, and it has wounded you, and it seems you have only one choice left.

Blood-stained porcelain bowl wobbles face down on woodfloor; orange peel not at all stirred by disbelieving last breath there among that fine summer dust-layer, fatal knife set down in passing-panic on familiar wobbly bannister, later dropped (thrown) by Mother (dear Mother) (heartsick) into the slow-flowing, chocolate-brown Potomac.

None of it was real; nothing was real.

Everything was real; inconceivably real, infinitely dear.

These and all things started as nothing, latent within a vast energy-broth, but then we named them, and loved them, and, in this way, brought them forth.

And now must lose them.

I send this out to you, dear friends, before I go, in this instantaneous thought-burst, from a place where time slows and then stops and we may live forever in a single instant.

Goodbye goodbye good—

roger bevins iii

CIV.

Caroline and Matthew and Richard and I lay entangled there in our spot near the flagpole: my part to Caroline's mouth, her rear to Richard's part, Matthew's part to my rear, Caroline's part being shared by Matthew's mouth and my extended stroking middle finger.

mr. leonard reedy

Seems we'd missed the big excitement.

mrs. caroline reedy

Having been engaged in some excitement of our own.

richard crutcher

But then, the noise of the many matterlightblooming phenomena growing annoying—

mrs. caroline reedy

We men became flaccid.

mr. leonard reedy

Making further excitement problematic.

mrs. caroline reedy

Me and Richard and Mr. Reedy hiked up our pants and Mrs. Reedy re-did her skirt and blouse and we rushed over along the fenceline toward that other (lesser) excitement.

matthew crutcher

En route we glimpsed Mr. Bevins—

mrs. caroline reedy

Damned nance.

richard crutcher

On his knees by the fence, mumbling to himself.

mr. leonard reedy

Then, the usual big to-do:
Flash of light, clothes raining down.

matthew crutcher

No more Bevins.

richard crutcher

CV.

The sun was nearly up.

Those of us who had survived that ghastly night huddled, conferred, went on brief sprinting expeditions, searching for survivors.

We did not find Purdy, nor Johannes, nor Crawley.

Did not find Pickler, Ella Blow, Verna Blow, Appleton, Scarry, Thorne.

Midden was missing, as were Goncourt, Cupp, Edwell, and Longstreet.

Reverend Thomas: missing.

Even Bevins and Vollman, two of our most long-standing and faithful residents: gone.

How we pitied these. So gullible. Broken by the rantings of a mere boy. Lost forever.

Sweet fools.

lance durning

Here we were. Were we not? If not, who spoke? Who heard?

percival "dash" collier

What a slaughter.

And we had only managed to survey a tiny fraction of the premises.

lance durning

Soon day began to break in earnest, and here came the usual all-body weakness, and the accompanying sense of diminishment, and we dashed off for our respective home-places, and situated ourselves squeamishly within our sick-forms, eyes closed or averted, so as not to see what those foul things had become.

robert g. twistings

And as the sun came up, we prayed, each within ourselves, our usual prayer:

lawrence t. decroix

To still be here when the sun next set.

mrs. antoinette boxer

And discover, in those first moments of restored movement, that we had again been granted the great mother-gift:

robert g. twistings

Time.

lance durning

More time.

percival "dash" collier

CVI.

As always at Sun's rising, the two realms Merg'd, and all that was true in Ours, became true in Theirs: all the Stones, Trees, Shrubs, Hills, Valleys, Streams, Pondlets, Marshes, Patches of Light & Shade, merg'd, and were the same Betwixt the two Environs, and you could not have told one Realm from the other.

Much that was New & Strange & Unnerving had occurr'd this night.

We Three Bachelors had watched it all unfold from On-High: safe, separate, & Free—the way we liked it.

I enjoined my young Charges that we must now beat a hasty Retreat to our Sick-boxes, & get Ourselves within.

Within that which Awaited us there.

stanley "perfesser" lippert

Faugh.

gene "rascal" kane

We did not like entering those things.

jack "malarkey" fuller

At all.

gene "rascal" kane

But *that* was the Price; we must abide, fully Awake but Inert, within those Foul Things that had once Resembled (aye, had once *Been*) us (&

which we had loved so Dearly) until such time as Night Again fell, at which time, shooting Forth, we would be—

stanley "perfesser" lippert

Free.

gene "rascal" kane

Free again.

jack "malarkey" fuller

Ourselves, truly.

gene "rascal" kane

All of Bless'd Creation restored to us.

stanley "perfesser" lippert

Everything again possible.

gene "rascal" kane

We Three had never Wed, nor truly Lov'd, but, once Night fell again, and if we found ourselves still Resident here, might strike the "never"—

stanley "perfesser" lippert

For until we are ended, "never" may not be truly said.

jack "malarkey" fuller

And love may yet be ours.

gene "rascal" kane

CVII.

Just now took lantern out to Carroll crypt Tom to make sure all was well and found young Lincoln's coffin slightly jutting out of the wallslot and pushed it back in oh that poor little fellow concluding his first ever lonely night here of many such lonely nights to come a long sad eternity of such nights.

Could not help but think of our Philip about same age as Pres's boy who will be racing about the yard and come in just positively lit up from inside with joy of living having been flirting over fence with the misses amy & reba leonard nextdoor his hair tousled and grab a broom and in his overflow of happy spirits goose Mrs Alberts the cook in her hind-quarters but when she turns to give him a wallop back holding a tremendous turnip and sees that glowing face what can she do but drop said turnip into washbasin and grabbing him about neck smother him with kisses while I secretly hand her broom so as he scats away victorious she can give him a sort of avenging goose of her own in his familiar play-worn trousers and a good poke too as that ladys arms are like pot roasts O Lord I cannot bear the thought of Philip lying still in such a place as this and when that thought arises must hum some scrap of tune energetically while praying No no no take that cup away Lord let me go first before any of them I love (before Philip Mary Jack Jr. before dear Lydia) only thats no good either since when they reach their end I will not be there to help them? O either way it is unbearable O God what a bind one is in down here Tom dear friend Tom I long for sleep I await your arrival, & hope these sad & morbid thoughts will soon fade away soon with the happy sight of our dear friend rising the Sun.

Manders, op. cit.

CVIII.

I rode along in that gentleman, upon our little horse, through those quiet streets, and I was not unhappy. Though he was. He had neglected his wife by this night's indulgence, he felt. And they had another little sick boy at home. Who might also succumb. Though he was better today, he might yet succumb. Anything could happen. As he now knew. He had forgotten. He had somewhat forgotten, about the other boy.

Tad. Dear little Tad.

The gentleman had much on his mind. He did not wish to live. Not really. It was, just now, too hard. There was so much to do, he was not doing it well and, if done poorly, all would go to ruin. Perhaps, in time (he told himself) it would get better, and might even be good again. He did not really believe it. It was hard. Hard for him. Hard for me. To be in there. I resolved nevertheless to stay. It was getting on near morning. Normally, during the day, we took our rest. Were drawn back to our shells and must rest in there. Tonight I did not feel that draw. But I was sleepy. I dozed, and slipped through him, into his horse, who was, I felt at that moment, pure Patience, head to hoof, and fond of the man, and never before had I felt oats to be such a positive thing in the world, or so craved a *certain blue blanket*. And then I roused myself, and sat up straight, and fully rejoined the gentleman.

And we rode forward into the night, past the sleeping houses of our countrymen.

thomas havens

ABOUT THE TYPE

This book was set in Fournier, a typeface named for Pierre-Simon Fournier (1712–1768), the youngest son of a French printing family. He started out engraving woodblocks and large capitals, then moved on to fonts of type. In 1736 he began his own foundry and made several important contributions in the field of type design; he is said to have cut 147 alphabets of his own creation. Fournier is probably best remembered as the designer of St. Augustine Ordinaire, a face that served as the model for the Monotype Corporation's Fournier, which was released in 1925.

GEORGE SAUNDERS

'One of the geniuses of 21st century fiction'
Guardian

'As slender as a psalm, and as heavy'
New York Times

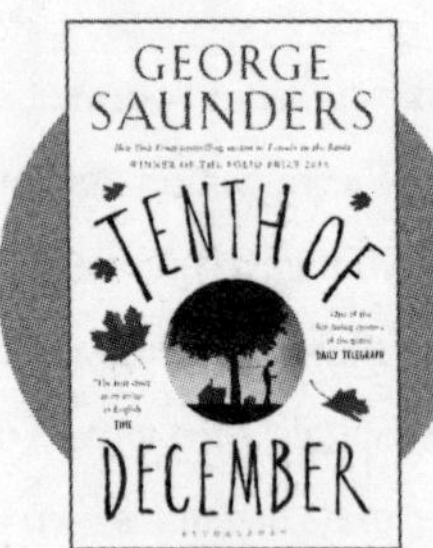

'Funny, poignant, deeply moving'
Hari Kunzru

'Not since Twain has America produced a satirist this funny'
Zadie Smith

'Surreal and puncturing'
Margaret Atwood

'A comic genius, with a depth, heart and tenderness all of his own'
Jon Ronson

'Just the kind of stories we need to get us through these times'
Thomas Pynchon